Book 2 in the
Among Fallen Angels Series

DEVIL'S POOL

TOM MORRIS

CHAPTER 1

Am I about to make the biggest mistake of my life?

Maria had been sitting in her classroom grading papers on a Friday afternoon. Now she leaned forward and put her head in her hands as the tears began to flow. Three years ago, Gabe had awakened passions in her she never knew she had and changed the direction of her life. But what about Brian? He was a good man. He was mature, reliable, and would make a great father to her future children. Maria also believed Brian was about to ask her to marry him. They had plans to go to the same local pizzeria they had gone to on their very first date. It was the perfect setting for Brian to propose.

But Maria couldn't stop thinking about Gabe's words when he unexpectedly came into her classroom moments earlier: "I had to see you again."

She had been convinced he was the one until she learned about his involvement in her father's illicit work as boss of the Philadelphia mafia. Gabe's prison sentence and disappearance into the federal witness protection program had made the decision for her. She had not seen or heard from him since. When Maria left the convent and took a teaching job at Saint Bart's School in Maple Grove, she found, much to her surprise, that Brian Murphy, a man she had dated in college, was a fellow teacher and assistant headmaster. With Gabe out of the picture, it didn't take long for her and Brian to settle into a comfortable relationship.

But should she settle for a "comfortable" relationship now that Gabe was back?

He had spoken only a few words to Maria in the classroom. He said he had thought about her every day for the past three years and wanted to explain "a lot of things" to her. When he had asked if he could see her again, she had sighed and said "I don't know." Then he was gone.

Should she see Gabe again when she was on the verge of receiving Brian's proposal? Wasn't Gabe in witness protection for a reason? Would he be willing to walk away from the kind of life he led when he worked for her father?

Maria could feel a headache coming on as she sat pondering. She needed some time not only to get better, but also to think things through before potentially receiving a marriage proposal. She picked up her phone and dialed.

"Hello," Brian said. "I was just thinking about you. What time shall I pick you up tonight?"

"I'm sorry, but I don't think I can go," Maria answered in a soft voice. "I'm getting a bad headache, and I think I just need to go home, take a pill, and rest."

"Are we still on for your niece's birthday party tomorrow night?" Brian asked with a sigh.

"I guess so," she almost whispered.

"I'll call you tomorrow. I hope you feel better." Brian hung up abruptly.

CHAPTER 2

The next evening, Maria and Brian pulled into her brother's drive-way in Chestnut Hill. Her parents had lived in the house before her father went to prison. Now that Raphael D'Angelo had succeeded his father as head of the family, the house belonged to him. Maria's father, Michael, had assured her she would be taken care of in the estate, but she didn't really care about the money or want anything.

Brian and Maria waited in the car as they were fourth in line for the valet.

"You're quiet tonight. Is everything okay?" Brian asked.

"I guess my headache last night really threw me for a loop. But I'm feeling a lot better now," Maria said. She really did feel better. Having a day to think things over had helped settle her mind. She had to admit that the thought of being with Gabe was exciting, and the heartbreak she felt after the trial hadn't totally disappeared, but she had grown to care for Brian and she couldn't conceive of abandoning their relationship to be with Gabe.

This was the first time Brian had been to the D'Angelo home in Chestnut Hill. He had met Maria's brother at a Christmas party, but he and Maria did not travel in the same circles as Raph.

"Do you feel strange coming here? I mean, knowing all about Raph's business?" Brian asked.

"Well, it's where I grew up, so it's not too strange, but things are different now with Raph. He's always cordial with me, but he seems cold somehow. Maybe the kinds of things he does has hardened his heart."

"Maybe you should just stop coming to these things," Brian said. "He lives in a different world, one we really don't want anything to do with."

"But he's family. And I've always loved Tessa. It's worth it just to see her. Besides, my mother is probably going to make an appearance." Maria had kept in close touch with her mother after her father went to prison. Carmella had been diagnosed with Parkinson's disease and had downsized into a condo. Maria went to visit her at least once a week. It wasn't easy for Carmella to get around, but she would always rouse herself to see her granddaughter, Tessa.

"I hope we don't have to stay too late," Brian said.

"We won't, but let's be polite and not leave too soon either."

When they reached the front of the valet line and got out, Maria could hear music coming from the back yard. Suddenly, she was struck with a memory of Tessa's party three years ago, when she had met Gabe. She could almost picture Gabe's handsome face under the lanterns illuminating the back yard. Maria paused, staring up at the front door.

"Everything okay?" Brian asked.

"Uh, yeah," she said hesitatingly as she took Brian's arm to walk up the front steps. When they got to the door, they were greeted by Rose, Raph's wife.

"Maria! It's so good to see you. You look wonderful!" Rose leaned in for a hug. "And this must be Brian. I think we met last Christmas."

"That's me," Brian said.

Rose gave him a hug, then led them through the living room to a porch that opened to the yard. Lanterns were once again strung on wires, giving the back yard a cozy, dimly lit appearance. Maria could see Raph sitting at a table with Gus Nasuti, an older man who had been a special advisor to her father and had somehow avoided prosecution when Michael D'Angelo and a number of his top underbosses had been arrested. It occurred to Maria there was no special table for Raph and his family since Raph had chosen to sit with his underbosses.

"You can sit with me," Rose said to Maria. "But first, let's tell the birthday girl you're here. Tessa, come see your Aunt Maria."

Tessa had been sitting at a table of young girls who were examining a Barbie doll with accessories, which must have been one of the gifts. She looked up and came running to embrace Maria in a hug.

"How's my favorite niece?" Maria asked.

"I'm your only niece," Tessa said with an emphatic voice.

"Happy birthday, my dear." Maria handed Tessa a gift bag. Maria felt a hand on her shoulder and turned to see Raph, who had left his table to come and greet her.

"Maria, I'm so glad you could come," he said, leaning in for a hug.

"Thanks. You know I'd never miss Tessa's party."

"I just sent someone over to pick up Mom," Raph said. "And you must be the headmaster at the school where Maria teaches," Raph said, looking at Brian.

"Actually, I'm no longer at Maria's school. I got a job at the public high school. I teach history and help coach football," Brian replied.

"He left Saint Bart's school about a year ago," Maria said, trying to keep the conversation going.

Someone tapped Raph on the shoulder, and he was gone as quickly as he had come.

"Well, your brother is as friendly as ever," Brian said. "I guess he's got a lot on his plate."

"You could say that," Maria said with a sigh. She glanced over at Rose, who was standing near Tessa and her friends. When they made eye contact, Rose beckoned Maria back to the table. Maria grabbed Brian by the arm and led the way.

"Brian, could you be a gentleman and get me a cosmopolitan from the bar? The same for you, Maria?" Rose asked. Maria nodded and Brian headed off. "Maria, I wanted to have a quick word with you before your mother arrives," Rose continued. "I hope it's not too upsetting, but I feel I need to tell you something."

"Sure, what is it?"

"I heard Raph talking on the phone the other day and I think Gabe has left witness protection."

"Really? How does he know that?" Maria asked, not revealing she had already seen him.

"I didn't hear the whole conversation because he was on the phone, but some of the guys that work for us saw Gabe in town. Apparently, he was in a bar near where Francesca's used to be."

"Does anyone know where he is now?" Maria asked.

"I don't think so. One of Raph's guys called him from the bar, but Gabe left, and no one saw where he went. Again, I hope this isn't too upsetting for you."

"I appreciate the information, but why are you telling me this?"

"I know you two were close before he was a key witness against our family," Rose said, "so I felt you should know. Gabe is in a lot of danger right now. I heard Raph say something about making an example of him, and you know what that means. You can't testify against a family like ours and get away with it."

Rose's disclosure confirmed what Maria had suspected for a while—that her sister-in-law's loyalty to Raph was starting to break down. "I don't think my father would approve of doing anything to Gabe," Maria said.

"Well, unfortunately, Raph is the new boss, and he doesn't always listen to your father. After your father lost his latest appeal, Raph is pretty sure he won't ever get out of prison."

"I don't know what to do," Maria said as she pulled a tissue out of her purse and began dabbing her eyes.

"If Gabe reaches out to you, tell him to go as far from Philadelphia as he can."

Brian arrived with the drinks. "Two cosmopolitans for the two most charming ladies at the party." As he spoke, there was some scattered applause as a male nurse in blue scrubs wheeled an older woman onto the back patio.

Maria and Rose trotted over and Rose took control of the wheelchair. "How're you doing, Mom?" Rose asked as Maria leaned over to kiss her mother on the cheek.

"I guess I'll be alive for at least another day or two," Carmella said sarcastically. As they wheeled Carmella to the table, Rose looked for Raph so he could greet his mother, but he was nowhere to be seen.

◆　◆　◆

While the festivities continued outside, Raph was in his home office with Gus Nasuti and two of his top captains, Lenny Rizzo and Phil Morino. "I pulled you guys in to tell you that yesterday I got a call from Jimmy from a bar downtown. He said he saw Gabriel Rossi in the bar."

"Which bar?" Lenny asked.

"Jack's on Lombard Street."

"I thought he was in witness protection," Phil said with a puzzled look on his face.

"Yeah, he was," Raph said. "I didn't tell you guys right away 'cause I wanted to make some calls to check the story out. I couldn't find out much, but it looks like Gabe flew the coop."

"You know what that means," Gus said. "The feds will be watching him to see if he goes back to his old ways. He might even have broken the conditions of his parole, so they may be looking to arrest him."

"Or just watching to see if he leads them to anything interesting," Lenny added.

"If we've seen him, it's possible others have seen him as well," Gus said. "So what are we going to do about it?"

"You know the rules, Gus," Raph answered. "We gotta deal with this. If we let the guy who put my father away go bar hopping around the city, nobody's going to respect us. At the same time, we gotta be super careful because the feds will be watching."

"So, you want me to set up a team to find him and take care of it?" Lenny asked.

"Let's think about it for a sec," Raph said. "You gotta wonder why he came back. He knows he's in danger here. What would make a guy like him come back?"

"Could be money. Maybe he's got a stash somewhere and he came to get pick it up," Phil suggested.

"But why show his face in public right on our doorstep?" Lenny asked. "Seems to me he'd quietly come in, collect his buried treasure, and get the hell out of here before anybody realized he was here."

"I know Gabe better than any of you. It wouldn't surprise me if he just missed his old stomping grounds and wanted to visit," Raph said. "Or maybe it was more of an 'in your face, catch me if you can' kinda thing. The only other reason I can think of is he came to see my sister." Raph took a sip from his glass of scotch. "Before Gabe was caught, they were getting quite close. Maria gave up on being a nun after she met him. In fact, when he got caught, he was spending the night with her at the cabin on Arrowpoint Lake."

"So if we find him, the feds may be watching since he's violated his parole. So what do we do?" Gus asked.

"We need to be extra careful. Hey, we ran a big gambling joint for years in South Philadelphia right under the Feds' noses and they never got wind of it until the Carbones attacked us and burned it down. I think we can handle a hit on a guy like Gabe," Raph said.

"I got to know Gabe pretty well myself," Gus said. "He's smart and he knows how to disappear when he doesn't want to be found. I think you need to put some manpower on finding him."

"Yeah, you're right. He is smart," Raph said. "But I think I've got an idea how we can catch him without attracting attention from the feds, and it won't take a lot of manpower."

◆ ◆ ◆

"Is your headache back again?" Brian asked as they drove home from the party. "Maybe you should see a doctor. Actually, maybe we should both see one. I've been getting more headaches than usual lately too."

"I've already been to a doctor and she prescribed my migraine pills," Maria snapped.

"Did someone say something to upset you at the party?"

"No, I'm fine. Just a little tired."

"Tired or not, you don't seem like yourself," Brian added. Maria didn't answer.

She felt bad for Brian. He was a good man and he didn't deserve to be treated like this. But after Gabe's surprise visit at her school and Rose telling her he was in danger since Raph knew he was in town, she couldn't stop thinking about Gabe. At first, Maria was angry at Gabe when he was arrested and she realized he had kept her in the dark about what he did for her father. Then again, her parents had kept her in the dark for most of her life, and she continued to love them. She was also upset when Gabe took the witness stand and testified about the criminal operations her father led. Now, three years later, she realized the evidence against her father was overwhelming and that his prison sentence was the result of a lifetime of criminal activity. When the FBI arrested Gabe, they seized his laptop, which was a treasure trove of information about the D'Angelo family and its crimes, especially the illegal gambling operations Gabe himself had supervised. They had him dead to rights, and he was facing decades in prison if he didn't cooperate.

Even though Maria struggled to forgive Gabe, she perceived that deep down, he was a good man. He had made some bad choices for sure, but she had seen the way he worked with kids when she invited him to an outing at the lake by the convent, and she saw the joy he displayed when he helped her at the soup kitchen. She was convinced that if he had the chance, he could walk away from a life of crime and lead a good, productive life. Part of Maria still wanted to help him do that.

"Here we are," Brian said, since Maria was staring ahead in a seemingly trance-like state.

"Oh, okay," she said as she grabbed her purse from the floor and prepared to get out.

"Can I pick you up for church tomorrow?" They both attended Saint Bart's, the church affiliated with the school where Maria taught.

"Uh, I guess so," Maria said with no enthusiasm.

"Tell you what. I'll call you in the morning and see how you're doing. I hope you get some good rest tonight," Brian said as he leaned in for a goodnight kiss. Maria turn her cheek to him for the kiss, then she slid out the door and walked up the steps to her townhouse.

CHAPTER 3

Gabe sat in the parking lot at a Dunkin Donuts in Hatboro, one of the northern suburbs of Philadelphia, just north of Maple Grove where Maria taught. It was a small town where the D'Angelo family had no business. He'd bought a coffee at the drive-thru window, not wanting to risk going into the shop. He'd learned his lesson when he went into a bar in South Philadelphia and recognized one of the patrons as a D'Angelo soldier. He knew it was stupid, but he just couldn't resist stopping into one of his favorite hangouts after being away for three years. Gabe assumed he'd been made, so he decided to get out of the city for a while. Someone knocked on the passenger side window. Gabe hit the unlock button and a bald, middle-aged man got in.

"Gabe. It's great to see you," the man said. "I was shocked when you called. I didn't think I'd ever see you again."

"Andy, you have no idea how glad I am to see you," Gabe said. Andy Carr ran a bookmaking operation in the northern suburbs. Several years ago, after hearing rumors that Andy was encroaching D'Angelo territory, Gabe had decided to check out the situation. He met Andy and concluded there was no truth to the rumors. The two hit it off and became friends, trading information and tips about the world of gaming and gambling. Once, Andy got in a pinch and needed ten thousand dollars to pay off a bet made by a guy in Doylestown with connections to the New Jersey mob. Gabe loaned Andy the money. Andy paid off the loan on time and their friendship was cemented forever.

"What the hell are you doing around here?" Andy asked. "I heard you were in witness protection."

"I was, but I've had enough." Gabe pulled another cup of coffee out of a bag and offered it to Andy. "I know it's risky coming around here, but I'm prepared to deal with it. Besides, I had to pick up some stuff I had in storage."

"Well, if there's anything I can do to help, just say the word." Andy took a sip of the coffee.

"There may be something. I know you have some rental properties around here and I was wondering if there was somewhere I could crash until things cool down. Don't worry, I can pay rent."

"I do have an empty condo close by. Don't worry about the rent. It's yours as long as you need it," Andy said. "You got me out of a real pinch once, and I always wanted to return the favor. If there's anything else I can do, just say so."

"Now that you mention it, I need to ditch this car and get something that can't be traced back to me."

"Didn't they give you a new identity in witness protection?"

"Yeah, they did. The car is registered under my new identity, so the Feds can still find me. I'd like to keep them at bay for a while."

"Sure thing, Gabe. I have some contacts who I'm sure can help you with that."

"Thanks, buddy. You are a true friend."

The list of people Gabe felt he could trust was a short one, and Andy was at the top of the list. Right now, the only other person on that list was Maria, and Gabe would reach out to her again soon enough.

Chapter 4

Special Agent Natalie Perez was the new head of the FBI Organized Crime Task Force at the Philadelphia Field Office. She had been a key player in the investigation that brought down Michael D'Angelo and several of his captains three years ago, which made her the obvious choice when the previous head, Leon Dempsey, retired a year ago. Agent Johnson Reed, another veteran of mafia investigations, was still on the Task Force, but he was also nearing retirement and was pretty much finished with field work. Reed assumed the role of an elder statesman, offering his input and comments at meetings. Agent Perez had called the meeting today to address some new developments in organized crime in the region.

Unlike Agent Dempsey, Agent Perez was usually the first to arrive for scheduled meetings. She sat at the head of the large table in the conference room as Reed and a half dozen younger agents filed in. At her right sat Special Agent Dennis McIntyre, her key assistant. Special Agent McIntyre stood and handed out briefing packages as the other agents filed in.

"Let's get started," Perez said unceremoniously. "I called this meeting to bring you up to date on some matters that are of interest to this task force. I've asked Special Agent McIntyre to report on the first item."

Agent McIntyre cleared this throat and signaled to an administrative assistant at the other end of the table who dimmed the lights and switched on a PowerPoint presentation. The first slide showed a photo of Gabriel Rossi.

"As some of you may recall, Gabriel Rossi was an up-and-coming soldier in the D'Angelo organization. Rossi had gained the confidence of his boss, Michael D'Angelo, and was successfully managing various gambling and sports betting operations in southeast Pennsylvania. When the D'Angelo family went to war with the Carbones, the D'Angelos got tipped off that the Carbones were planning to kidnap Michael D'Angelo's daughter, Maria. Maria was living in a convent in Lindenwood, Pennsylvania. Michael D'Angelo asked Rossi to protect Maria and take her to a safe location. The FBI received a tip that the Carbones had three soldiers following Rossi and Maria to a safe house in the Poconos. As I'll explain later, we're not certain, but we believe that the tip-off came from within the Carbone organization from sources who didn't like the idea of taking action against Michael D'Angelo's family members."

Agent McIntyre picked up his cup of coffee and took a sip. "Are you with me so far?" The agents around the table nodded. "Fortunately, we got to the safe house in time to prevent the kidnapping. However, just as we arrived, Rossi killed one of the Carbone's operators and was seriously wounded himself. Our team was fired on by another Carbone soldier who was guarding the rear of the house and was killed by our return fire."

Agent McIntyre called for the next slide, which showed the crime scene at the safe house. "Our team entered the open front door and Rossi and the intruder were both unconscious on the floor. We determined the intruder was dead but Rossi was still alive. Ms. D'Angelo was also present and was taken into protective custody."

"Did the FBI team know her identity when you found her?" one of the agents asked.

"Agent Perez questioned her and learned her identity. It appeared she was not involved in the gun battle, and a field kit was used to determine there was no gunshot residue on her hands. We placed Rossi under arrest and he was kept under guard at the hospital. You'll notice the open laptop in plain view on the coffee table in front of the sofa in the slide. This was the key to breaking open the case against Michael D'Angelo and many of his captains. It contained information on the illegal gambling operations throughout the organization, including location, size, revenues, and key personnel. It also contained the bookkeeping records prepared by Diane D'Angelo, Michael D'Angelo's niece. Among other things, she ran high stakes poker games in the back of a restaurant in South Philadelphia.

"Rossi's fingerprints were all over the laptop, so there's no question that it was his. There were also notations on the laptop about a hit on one of the Carbones. Rossi made it clear that he had been asked to assist in the hit but was pulled off the job at the last minute. Suffice it to say, this twenty-nine-year-old soldier had enough offenses to put him away for decades. When Rossi recovered, he decided to cooperate in return for a short prison sentence—one year followed by five years of probation. By the time he recovered from his gunshot wound, he only had a few months left to serve in prison."

"Don't you think it's unusual that Rossi documented so much criminal activity that he could be tied to?" one of the agents asked.

"The short answer is yes, it is unusual. However, from his point of view, the records also show what a good job he was doing managing the gambling operations that he oversaw. Maybe he was creating records of his successes to help him get made in the organization. In fact, that's what he told our investigators. As for the notation on the hit and his being pulled off, he no doubt wanted some exculpatory evidence to eliminate or reduce his involvement in a murder in case he got arrested. In fact, we did not charge him with murder or conspiracy, even though there was some evidence he participated in the conspiracy."

"Were the records on Rossi's computers comprehensive, covering all of the D'Angelo gambling operations?" Agent Reed asked.

"It's hard to say. The records were pretty comprehensive, but they focused on the things that Rossi was in charge of. We have reason to believe that Michael D'Angelo's son, Raphael, was also involved in the gambling operations but the records on Rossi's computer didn't cover that. Of course, Raphael is now the boss of the whole organization. It will be challenging, but hopefully we'll be able to gather more information on Raphael's involvement before he became the boss.

"You can read more details about Rossi's arrest, the evidence against him, and his testimony at the trial in the materials you received," Agent McIntyre continued. "The important point for today is that Rossi was set up in the witness protection program with a job as a tennis instructor and an apartment in West Proctor, Missouri. Yesterday, we received notification from the field office in Kansas City that Rossi missed a meeting with his supervisor in the Witness Protection Program and he has not returned to his apartment in the past six days. Of course, his car is missing."

"So how does this relate to us?" one of the agents asked.

"I'll get to that," Agent McIntyre replied, then asked for the next slide. "Here is a toll booth image of Rossi in his car on the Heart of America Bridge, crossing over into Kansas City, Kansas. That's the only image we've been able to find as of this time."

"So does this indicate he's heading west?" one of the agents asked.

"That's a possibility. But in cases such as this, it's not unusual for the subject to make some diversionary moves to mislead us. Rossi lived his entire life in Philadelphia. It's where his friends and family members live. He may even have a stash of money or contraband here that he needs to get to. It would be easy for him to double back on less travelled roads to avoid detection."

"Has a warrant been issued for his arrest?" Agent Reed asked.

"Right now, our goal is to find him before the D'Angelo family does. If he's in the area, we'll pick him up and bring him in on a VOP.

In the meantime, we know that Rossi lived in a townhouse at Fifth and Catherine Streets and he spent much of his working and personal time in that neighborhood. It seems like a natural place for him to return to, so I've asked a number of you to check CCTV footage over the past two weeks within a ten-block radius."

"That's a pretty large area," one of the younger agents observed.

"It certainly is, but it encompasses the area where Rossi lived and worked, so there's a good chance we'll get some hits if he's back in town, and hopefully that will help us narrow our search."

Agent Perez had been quiet up to this point. "Rossi must know that we won't be the only ones looking for him. Once word gets out that he may be in the area, I'm sure the D'Angelos will be looking for him as well. He's in a lot of danger. That's why we want to see where he is and possibly where he leads us. At the same time, we won't let him hang out there long enough to become a victim of the D'Angelo family's revenge.

"Thank you, Agent McIntyre for your presentation," Perez continued. "We're putting out an alert for all agents in the region to be on the lookout. The New Jersey field offices have done the same. So, let's not limit ourselves to the CCTV cameras. Get out and beat the bushes; check with some of your informants to see if there's any word on the street about Rossi's whereabouts," Perez ordered before adjourning the meeting.

CHAPTER 5

After getting settled into his apartment in Warminster, Gabe decided to risk a drive over to Margate, New Jersey. He felt he had to confirm certain rumors he had heard. He had managed to get an audience with Hank Maranzano, the boss of the mafia in southern New Jersey. Maranzano took over after the death of Bruno Carbone three years ago, and Gabe had heard he had been behind the killing of Carbone, who had ordered the kidnapping of Maria. There were other rumors Gabe wanted to ask about as well.

It wasn't easy convincing Maranzano to meet with him—after all, Gabe had ratted out his own boss, Michael D'Angelo. That's a cardinal sin in the mafia world. Hank had been friendly with Michael, and the D'Angelo family had breathed a sigh of relief when he took over because it had lessened the violent conflict between the two families. But now that Raphael was in charge in Philadelphia, the relationship had soured. Gabe's only hope was that he had some valuable information to offer the New Jersey boss.

Maranzano had agreed to meet Gabe at an outdoor café a few blocks from the beach in Margate. The meeting was in broad daylight, and Gabe knew Maranzano's bodyguards would be close by watching. He hoped the FBI would not be watching, although he had switched cars and changed his appearance somewhat by cutting his thick, dark hair to crew-cut length, dying it a lighter color, and growing a mustache. It wasn't a total makeover, but enough to confuse someone watching from a distance.

Gabe sat at the prescribed table, and in a few minutes a black Cadillac Escalade pulled up and several men got out. One opened the rear door for Maranzano. Gabe had not seen him in a long time, but there was no mistaking who was walking toward him. Hank signaled the other men to get back in the car, which pulled a few feet away and parked. Maranzano took a seat at the table.

"I don't know why I agreed to do this," Maranzano said. "I guess I was impressed you had the balls to meet me in public after what you did to Michael."

"Hank, I'm not here to debate what I did or didn't do. I think it's pretty obvious that I had no choice. I was almost killed by your guys, or Carbone's guys I guess, and the FBI found enough on my laptop to convict me and Michael whether I testified or not. They offered me a deal I couldn't refuse. If I hadn't taken it, I would have been in prison for most of my life," Gabe said. "I wouldn't have been caught if Carbone hadn't decided to kidnap Maria."

Maranzano looked at Gabe with a cold stare. "Okay, so what do you got for me that's worth me coming to this meeting? It better be good."

"I've got a question, then I'll give you some information that could be very valuable to you," Gabe said.

"Okay, what's your question?"

"The D'Angelos went to great length to keep Maria out of the business and to keep her life private. Somebody must have tipped off the Carbones about her, where she was and what she was doing. Who was it?" Gabe asked.

"Before I even consider answering your question, I need to know who your information is about to see if I'm even interested in it." Maranzano replied.

Gabe grimaced. He didn't want to give any details until he got the information he was looking for, but Maranzano had outmaneuvered him. Gabe decided he had been lucky to get this meeting and that he would probably never have the chance to speak to the New Jersey boss again.

"Okay. I've got enough evidence on Raph to put him away for a long time."

"You never gave this to the FBI or the police?" Maranzano asked.

"They never asked me about Raph. They were totally focused on Michael and his top captains."

"So, what am I going to do with your information?" Maranzano asked, taking a sip of the iced tea the waiter had brought him without asking.

"That's up to you. You don't have the greatest relationship with Raph. His casinos are still in competition with your operations in Atlantic City. You never know when it might come in handy. It could give you leverage in a negotiation if it ever came to that."

"How did you get this information?"

"I worked closely with Raph on sports betting. He was kind of my boss. I usually went to him with problems before bothering Michael. His name is all over everything. I've even got a bank account he used, and a list of everyone else working with him on sports betting."

"Word on the street is Raph has a contract out on you. Won't this make him more determined to whack you?" Hank said with a chuckle.

"He won't know unless you use it. And if you do use it and leak it to the FBI, they'll take him into custody."

There was silence as Maranzano gestured for the waiter to give him a refill on his drink. Gabe pulled a small flash drive out of his pocket. "So, are you going to tell me who tipped Carbone off about Maria?"

"It was no one on our side. We wouldn't have known where Michael's daughter was unless someone close to her gave us the information. Let's just say it's someone you know. and that Bruno was surprised this person was willing to tip our guys off. He asked us to make sure she didn't get hurt, which worked for Bruno. Michael D'Angelo was the one he wanted to hurt."

"So, you're not going to give me a name?" Gabe asked.

"I think you know enough to figure it out."

Gabe thought for a moment and looked perplexed. "It was Raph who gave your guys the information?"

Maranzano leaned back and took another swallow of his tea. "I'm not going to say any more."

Gabe realized Maranzano had told him it was Rafael D'Angelo without mentioning any names. Raph had set in motion a plot to kidnap his own sister, and he nearly got Gabe killed in the process.

"But somebody also tipped the FBI off about the kidnapping. Was that you or one of your guys?" Gabe asked.

"No. We'd never tip the feds off about our own operation."

They both stared at their half-empty glasses for a minute.

"So do I get the info or not?" Maranzano asked.

"Sure. Here it is." Gabe dropped the flash drive on the table as he got up to leave.

"Be careful, Gabe. I know you were a victim of circumstances." Maranzano said with uncharacteristic kindness.

Now Gabe was really perplexed. Not only had Raph tipped off the Carbones where to find Maria, but when they went after her, he also tipped off the Feds? Raph knew Gabe was guarding her, so Raph could have figured Gabe would get caught. But why would Raph want to get Gabe caught by the FBI?

◆　◆　◆

On the drive back to his borrowed apartment, Gabe realized if he made good time, he could probably catch Maria at school before she left to go home. He didn't feel right about the way he left things when he visited her less than a week ago. He wanted to see her, to be with her, and spend time explaining things to her. He decided not to tell her outright that her brother had betrayed her. She probably wouldn't have believed him anyway. Gabe could hardly believe it himself, but he had gotten a clear message from Hank Maranzano, who had no reason to lie about it as far as Gabe could tell.

On the drive, Gabe went a little out of his way to avoid the traffic in the city and got on the Pennsylvania Turnpike. He got off the Maple Grove exit about four o'clock, figuring Maria would probably be at the school a little while longer. A few minutes later, he pulled into the parking lot behind the school. He was right. Maria's car was one of the last in the lot, parked under the shade of a maple tree. Gabe parked a few spaces away and decided to wait in his car until she came out. No more surprise visits when she was alone, or nearly alone, in the building.

After waiting about fifteen minutes, Gabe saw Maria leave through the rear entrance of the building. When she was about twenty feet from her car, Gabe got out and stood between their cars. "Maria," he said.

Maria stared at him with a puzzled look. "Gabe, is that you?"

"Yes. I'm sorry to approach you this way, but I need to speak to you for a moment."

"You look different."

"Yeah, I got a haircut and grew a mustache." Gabe didn't go into the reasons for the change. "I'm sorry to bother you. Is there a place we could speak in private? I promise I won't take much of your time."

"I don't know if that's a good idea. I'd better get home," she said, opening her car door and throwing her bag into the passenger seat.

"Then just hear me out for a minute."

Maria closed the door and leaned against the car, crossing her arms.

"First," Gabe said, "I want to tell you how sorry I am."

"For what?"

"For everything. I'm sorry I misled you about my job for your father. And I'm sorry I didn't do a better job of protecting you at the cabin. If there is any way I can make it up to you, I will."

"There's no need. You kept me from getting kidnapped, and you almost got killed in the process," she said.

"Then there was the trial. I know I caused you and your family a lot of heartache."

"Well, it's clear to me now that my father was involved in criminal activities. But it still hurts when I think of the role you played in it, and that you were also involved."

"Maria, believe me. I'm sorry that I misled you. Of course, if I had told you everything at the start, I don't know if we would have gotten to know each other. Again, I wish there was some way I could make it up to you."

"The best way you could make it up to me would be to leave that way of life."

"I'm trying to do that." The two were silent for a few moments before Gabe spoke again. "Your father was my boss, but he was also a good friend to me. They had evidence to put your father and me away for a long time. They could have done that even if I didn't testify. My testimony just made the trial shorter, and when they offered me a deal that would get me out of prison in less than a year, what could I do?" Gabe looked down. "If you can't accept that, I understand."

"Why are you here? Aren't you supposed to be in witness protection?"

"Yes, but I got tired of pretending to be someone I'm not. I couldn't spend my life away from my hometown and everything I've always known," Gabe said. "And what I said to you in the classroom—"

Maria interrupted him. "But you're in danger, Gabe. Raph's wife, Rose, told me I should warn you if I ever saw you. If you want to stay safe, you should get far away from here." Maria's eyes teared up.

"I'm fully aware of the danger I'm in," Gabe said. "To be honest, you're the main reason I came back. I've thought about you every day. Maybe there's no chance you'll want to be with me, but I had to try." He walked closer and took Maria in his arms, surprised that she didn't resist.

"Gabe, I understand what you had to do, but my life is different now. It's been three years, and I had no idea where you were. I've been seeing someone, and I think he wants to marry me."

"I'm not going to give up on you," Gabe said as he continued to hold her. "I missed you while I was away."

"I missed you as well. But I didn't think I'd ever see you again, so I moved on."

While Maria and Gabe spoke, Brian got out of his car in the front parking lot. He had planned to surprise Maria with a dinner invitation. He walked up and tried the front doors of the school, but they were locked. He turned and walked toward the closest corner to go around and try the rear doors the teachers used to enter and exit the building. As he turned the corner, he saw Maria in the arms of a man he didn't recognize. The man was caressing her back with his hands; Maria rested her head on his shoulder. This was an affectionate embrace. Brian stood with his mouth open, expecting the hug to end. When it didn't, he turned and walked back toward the front parking lot. The man wasn't anyone from the school, since he knew everyone who worked there. He knew about Gabe, how he had become close to Maria, and how he was severely wounded trying to protect her. Was it Gabe who was embracing the woman he wanted to marry? Wasn't Gabe gone forever after being put in witness protection? Then again, at one point Saturday evening, he thought he heard Rose mention Gabe to Maria, but he didn't hear any of the conversation. Was Gabe back in town?

Brian felt nauseous in the pit of his stomach. Maybe this was all a misunderstanding, he hoped. But when he thought about the long embrace and caressing, he doubted there was any misunderstanding. He couldn't imagine Maria cheating on him. If she wanted to leave him for someone else, surely she would be honest and up-front with him; that's the way she was. But then why was she in this clearly affectionate embrace? Brian got back in his car and slammed the door shut. He wanted to get away from the school and the town of Maple Grove, so he began driving to Glenside, where there was a tavern owned by the family of one of his high school friends. Brian felt confused, hurt, and more than a little angry. He looked forward to a double shot of bourbon and a friendly voice behind the bar to help him deal with the situation.

◆　◆　◆

Gabe ended the embrace and looked in Maria's eyes. "I know you've got some difficult choices, but I'm patient. I'll be here for you."

Maria tearfully stepped back from Gabe. "We really shouldn't do this. We can't just pick up where we left off three years ago. Things are different now for both of us. And I'm worried about your safety. Maybe you should leave. Where have you been staying?"

"I think it's better that you don't know. It's not far, but I don't want you to be in a position where you could be pressured to tell someone where I am."

"Gabe, I'd never tell anyone."

"I trust you, I just don't want to put you in that situation. And be careful around Raph. You shouldn't trust him."

"Really? Why not? He's my brother. I wouldn't call us close, but we get along."

"Maria, just trust me on this for now. There are things I need to talk to you about, but don't worry. Like I said, I'm here for you. If you need to reach me, you can call me on this." Gabe handed Maria a burner phone. "The only number in the contacts is mine. I can call you or leave a message on this phone as well."

"Why do I need to worry about someone tracing my calls?" Maria asked.

"You know the danger I'm in. I'll tell you more when we have a chance to talk again. I won't keep you in the dark like I did before."

"I understand you mean well, Gabe, but I just don't think I can do this. I'm practically engaged to a good man, I can't just walk away from that."

"I understand. All I'm asking for is some time with you, and a chance to talk again." Maria looked at Gabe without saying anything. She leaned in and kissed his cheek. "I'll take that as a 'maybe,'" Gabe said.

Maria's phone rang and she picked up. "What? Really? Where? Which hospital?" After a pause, she spoke again. "Okay, I'll be there as soon as I can." Maria hung up and looked at Gabe. "That was Raph. My mother has been rushed to the hospital."

She got in her car and drove off before Gabe could respond. As much as he wanted to be present for Maria, he knew the hospital was off limits. Raph was there, and some of his soldiers were probably close by as well. If he went, he'd be walking into a death trap. Gabe had been friendly with Carmella when he worked for Maria's father. He always admired her and felt Maria had inherited many good qualities from her. Gabe was exhausted after driving to Margate for the stressful meeting with Hank Maranzano. He decided he'd better get home and get some rest; he would call Maria in the morning to see how her mother was doing.

As Gabe got in his car, two men watched from a parked car across the street. One, Phil Morino, had binoculars.

"Look at that. Raph was right. She led us right to Rossi," Phil said to Tony Marriani, his driver.

"You sure it's Gabe? He looks different than I remember," Tony said.

"It's him all right. Let's get ready to move." Phil rolled up the passenger side window. Tony was the top driver in the D'Angelo family and he knew how to follow a car without being made. They tailed Gabe north on Easton Road until they reached Warminster, a little borough just outside of Hatboro. Tony made a couple right turns and entered a condo complex called "The Forest."

"Some forest," Tony joked. "I don't see no trees."

"Pay attention to your target," Phil snapped, failing to see the humor.

The complex consisted of several buildings containing five or six units each, with half on the ground level and half upstairs.

"He's going into building number four," Phil said as he stared through his binoculars. "Let's park here. Looks like he used a key fob to get in the main door."

"I just saw a light go on in the upstairs unit facing the front parking lot," Tony said.

"Good catch. That narrows it down. Now, if we can figure out which unit faces the street."

"Call Louie back at the clubhouse. He can look up the complex online and give us the unit number."

In less than five minutes, Phil, with help from the clubhouse, had identified Gabe's apartment as unit 4201. They also had the license plate on the nondescript gray Toyota Corolla Gabe had been driving.

"Time to call the boss," Phil said. He dialed a number and waited.

"Yeah?" Raph answered.

"How's your mother?" Phil asked.

"Not good. She's in intensive care. They think she had a bad stroke. How 'bout your project? Any luck?"

"He went to see Maria just like you said. We followed him home and we're looking at his condo. He just went inside. What do you want us to do?"

"Let's watch him a while. Stick the GPS tracker on his car. Maybe he'll lead us to something interesting."

A few minutes later, Tony put on a Papa John's Pizza shirt with a baseball cap and sunglasses to cover his face. He picked up a pizza box from the back seat and began walking across the parking lot. When he got to Gabe's car, he pretended to trip and drop the pizza box. When he bent down to pick it up, he was shielded from view. Tony slipped the magnetic tracker under Gabe's car, got up, dusted himself off, and continued walking with his empty pizza box. He continued to the building past Gabe's, put the box in a dumpster, then walked back to the car where Phil was staring at an open laptop.

"The tracker is up and running," Phil said. "Raph wants us to remain in the area for a few hours and see if he goes anywhere. We can go get a coffee or something. If Gabe starts to move, we'll follow him. We'll knock off at midnight and head home if he doesn't move."

CHAPTER 6

At about seven o'clock, Raph stood with Maria at their mother's bedside in the intensive care unit at Chestnut Hill Hospital. Carmella was unconscious as she lay among a variety of monitoring devices and tubes giving her oxygen and fluids. A nurse arrived to check on things and punched in some information on a computer. After checking Carmella's wrist band, she injected medicine into the intravenous port taped to her wrist. As soon as Maria had arrived, Raph's wife, Rose, had stepped out as only two visitors at a time were allowed.

"Have you spoken to the doctor yet?" Maria asked.

"I got here a half hour before you and he hasn't come in yet. The nurse says she had a bad stroke."

"What about Dad? Does he know?" Maria asked.

"I sent a message through legal channels. Bobby Sandone can get through a lot quicker than we can," Raph said.

Carmella was separated from Michael—not just by the fact that he was in prison; she had moved out of the house before the trial. Even though her parents were separated, Maria knew her father cared about Carmella and would want to know about her condition.

Maria shook her head and sighed. She gently put her hand on her mother's hand. "Mom, can you hear me? It's Maria." Tears started to form in her eyes. Carmella was unresponsive. "What about Father Pierce, has anyone called him?"

"I hadn't thought of that. Why don't you call him?"

"Okay, but the church is probably closed now. I'll have to call Henry to see if he has a direct number." Henry was Carmella's hired caregiver. Maria left to make the calls in the waiting room area.

"Any change?" Rose asked when Maria entered the waiting room. Rose looked distraught and had obviously been crying.

"No, I don't think so."

The two hugged.

"The nurse just told me the doctor is coming around soon. It's Dr. Harvey, Mom's private doctor. I think we should all be together to hear what he says," Rose said with a trembling voice.

"Of course. I'll just be a moment. I need to get a message to Father Pierce."

Maria was always struck by how close Rose had become to Carmella. Now she was even calling her "Mom." At first, Maria was a little put off by this, sometimes thinking Rose was closer to her mother than she was. But Maria came to accept Rose's relationship, knowing Rose had grown up without much of a family life. She was glad Rose could be there for Carmella when she was not available and she felt sorry for Rose, knowing how difficult it was to be married to someone in Raph's position.

Maria made her calls. She didn't particularly care for Father Pierce. She felt he pandered to her mother. And, of course, she couldn't forget how he reported her to the convent when she attended a party at her mother's home wearing makeup and perfume. But Father Pierce was her mother's priest, and Carmella wouldn't want anyone else if she could make the choice. Just as Maria ended her call and returned to her mother's room, Dr. Harvey came in.

"Are you here for Mrs. D'Angelo?" he asked.

"Yes," Rose and Maria said together.

"Let me have a look at her and we'll talk." Dr. Harvey spent about five minutes looking at Carmella's chart, listening to her heart and lungs, and shining a light on her eyes to examine the pupils.

The doctor came out with Raph and spoke to the small group. "Mrs. D'Angelo had a pretty severe ischemic event affecting her brain. That means she had a bad stroke."

"Is she going to be okay?" Rose asked.

"In her condition, with Parkinson's, it's hard to say. We don't know how much this stroke affected her brain. She's not very old, so you never know. If she wakes up in the next day or so, that's a good sign, but this can drag on for a few days. People with strokes like this can recover, although they may have difficulty talking and walking. You should prepare yourselves. I'm sorry I can't be more specific. I'll be around early in the morning. You can stay if you wish, but you should consider going home for some rest. We'll call if there's any change."

With that, the doctor left. Nobody wanted to go home, so they all stayed. A half hour later, Father Pierce arrived. Maria and Raph gave him an update on Carmella's condition.

"Are you going to administer last rites?" Rose asked.

"Yes, in a manner of speaking. I'm going to perform the Anointing of the Sick."

"So giving her last rites won't interfere with her possible recovery?" Raph asked.

"No, it doesn't work that way. I'll anoint her with oil and say the prescribed prayers. If the Lord chooses to heal her, that will be a great blessing. If not, this is how we prepare her for the next world," Father Pierce explained. "Either way, we're committing her into God's hands."

Maria reached in her purse and pulled out her rosary as she stood beside Father Pierce and began to whisper her own tearful prayers. Father Pierce dipped his finger in a small jar of oil and made the sign of the cross on Carmella's forehead, then said a prayer and pronounced a blessing.

"If she regains consciousness, or if there is any other change, please let me know," Father Pierce said. He nodded goodbye to the three and left. Maria and Rose wept for a few moments while Raph stood with his hands clasped, looking at his mother with a sad expression.

◆　◆　◆

Raph excused himself and left Rose and Maria in the intensive care area. He was about to go for some coffee when his phone rang. It was not a number he recognized.

"Raph," said a voice.

"Yeah, who is this?"

"It's Hank Maranzano. Look, I want to tell you how sorry I am about your mother. I used to know her when I worked with your father. She was a fine lady."

"You shouldn't say she *was* a fine lady. She's still with us and she could recover," Raph said, sounding a little annoyed.

"Point well taken. Just wanted you to know she's in our thoughts."

"Well, thanks for calling," Raph replied, eager to end the call.

"While I've got you," Hank said, "I had a visitor the other day. Gabe Rossi."

"What? Where is he?"

"He's gone and I don't know where he is."

"How come you let him go? You know he ratted out our family."

"Well, he just made a friendly call and he told me he's got information on you that could cause a lot of trouble with the FBI," Hank said, not mentioning the flash drive Gabe had given him.

Raph was about to say Gabe didn't have long to live when he remembered the call might be recorded. He never knew who was listening.

"What kind of information are you talking about?"

"Some kind of business records. He didn't give a lot of details. I think it had something to do with sports betting."

Raph felt a wave of nausea. He knew from the trial that Gabe kept detailed records he had no business keeping. "It's probably bullshit," Raph said. "Look, I gotta go. I'm at the hospital."

Raph disconnected the call.

◆　◆　◆

Raph sat next to his mother, seething with anger. He had volunteered to stay a few hours longer and sent Rose home with Maria. About one o'clock in the morning, he decided he was done playing games with Gabe. He couldn't stop thinking about the possibility of Gabe revealing things that could get him arrested. Raph stepped back into the waiting area and pulled out his phone.

"Don't you ever sleep?" the voice on the other end asked.

"Phil, change of plans. I want you to get rid of Gabe, and I mean now."

"Raph, I'm sorry, but we left more than an hour ago. I'm home and I sent Tony home after he dropped me off at the clubhouse. I can't handle this alone. I need someone with a different skill set to help me out. Maybe Denny Delvato."

"Then you and Denny get the hell over there!" Raph screamed.

"Raph, we know where he is. How 'bout I call Denny and we'll be over there at the crack of dawn. We'll do better with a few more hours' sleep," Phil said.

Raph wouldn't tolerate many of his captains speaking to him this way, but Phil was his right-hand man, so he let it go.

"Okay. But I want this done, and quickly."

"We're on it, boss. Why is this so urgent now? I thought we were gonna watch him and see what he's up to."

"I think I already found out what he's up to. Hank Maranzano called me tonight and he says Gabe's got information that could still bring us down."

"Didn't Gabe already spill everything to the feds?" Phil asked.

"Looks like he was holding back." Raph paused. "After you're done, I want you to search his place high and low and bring back anything you can find—files, flash drives, any stuff he might use against us. Bring anything valuable that you find too. Call me when it's done. I'm expecting to hear from you soon."

CHAPTER 7

Gabe sat at the little kitchen table with a cup of coffee he had brewed. It was only a few minutes after six, but he was eager to go out for a run. Gabe glanced out the window and saw the sun was shining without a cloud in the sky. It had taken a long time for him to recover from his gunshot wounds, and it was so hot and humid in Missouri for much of the year he had almost given up running. Gabe checked the headlines on his tablet, looking for any news about himself. Apparently, an ex-convict who went AWOL from the witness protection program wasn't newsworthy—at least not yet.

Gabe strapped a small Ruger .380 in a waistband holster under his shirt. He couldn't help thinking about the story of Salvatore Testa, the son of a former Philadelphia mafia leader who was executed while jogging in the New Jersey Pine Barrens one morning. Gabe would be ready if any of the D'Angelos were lucky enough to find him. He decided it was best to keep to the main roads where other people would be riding or travelling on foot.

There was a knock at the door.

Gabe stood up and unholstered his gun. He tiptoed over and stood to the side of the front door. He paused, took a deep breath, and yelled, "Who is it?"

"It's me, Andy. You said you were having trouble with the drain in the kitchen. I was out early and thought I'd swing by to check on it."

Gabe breathed a sigh of relief. "You're out awfully early. How'd you know I'd be up?"

"I can come back another time if it's too early."

"No, this is fine. I was just about to go for a run. Do you mind if I'm not here?" Gabe asked as he opened the door and Andy slipped in with a toolbox and a small bag from Home Depot.

"No. Go enjoy your run. I'll lock the door when I leave," Andy said.

"Thanks, Andy. I really appreciate this. There's some coffee in the pot if you want to pour yourself a cup."

"Don't mind if I do. I should be done in about a half hour."

"Okay. I probably won't be back by then. But thanks for everything. You're a good friend."

Gabe grabbed a baseball cap and some sunglasses to make it harder to recognize him and he was out the door. He turned out of his building's parking lot and trotted toward the back gate of the complex. He ran onto a side street that would lead him to York Road, one of the main thoroughfares in the area. He planned to head south three or four miles to Maple Grove, where he thought he would do a very careful run past Maria's school and see if her car was there. Even with being hunted by a mafia family and no doubt being sought by the FBI, Gabe felt more exhilarated than he had in a long time. Being in his hometown near Maria had a lot to do with that. He recalled the warmth of her embrace in the parking lot the other day and how worried she seemed for his safety. She had even said "I missed you." Gabe didn't know much about Maria's new boyfriend, but he felt deep down he still held a place in her heart. If he was patient, her current relationship might not work out, and he could be with her.

Gabe had a million and a half dollars he had pulled out of a storage unit in South Philadelphia and placed in another storage unit closer to where he was staying. It wasn't the kind of treasure you'd leave in an apartment anyone could break into. Gabe would need this money to start his new life and was already pondering several ideas. He usually did his best thinking when he was out running.

◆　◆　◆

Ten minutes after Gabe left, Phil and Denny rolled up in a nondescript Ford Explorer, a model that wouldn't look out of place at the complex.

"There's his car by building four. According to the tracker feed, he hasn't moved all night," Phil said, pointing his finger. "Let's park on the other side of the main entrance."

"I'll back in so we can leave quickly if we need to," Denny said. After backing into the spot, Denny screwed a suppressor onto the barrel of a compact Glock nine-millimeter pistol and tucked it into a special holster under his jacket. Then he pulled out a small bag with some tools to pick the lock on Gabe's door if he needed to.

"Let's do this," Phil said.

They got out of the car and began walking toward the front entrance.

CHAPTER 8

Maria had gone to the hospital early. On the drive over, she called the school and they told her not to worry, they would find someone to cover her class. She had offered to pick up Rose on the way, but she wasn't ready and said she would drive herself over in a little while. When Maria pulled into the parking garage at the hospital, it struck her that she hadn't spoken to Brian yesterday and that he probably didn't know her mother was in the hospital. She decided to make a quick call before going in.

"Brian?" she said when he picked up.

"That's me," he said somewhat sarcastically.

"You didn't call yesterday."

"Oh, it must have slipped my mind."

"What do you mean? You call every day."

"Like I said, it must have slipped my mind."

"Well, I'm sorry I didn't call you last night, but my mother is in the hospital. She had a stroke and she's in intensive care. I was there late with Raph and Rose. I'm going to see her again right now."

"I'm sorry to hear that. How is she?"

"I haven't heard anything, so I guess no news is good news. I'll get an update when I go in. If you want to visit, I can meet you here after school."

"I'm not sure if I can make it. They asked me to help with off-season weight training for our football players. Tonight is my turn to supervise."

"Couldn't you find someone to cover for you?"

"I don't think so. Actually, Maria, I've got to go. I'm running late and am hitting some traffic," Brian said and hung up.

Maria sat in the car and put her head down on the steering wheel. *Why was Brian so abrupt?* She really wanted him to come. She needed him now. Was it because she had been abrupt with him a few days ago? She didn't want to leave things with him this way, so she texted, "Sorry you couldn't talk. I really do need to talk to you. I'll call or text when I find out how my mother is doing. I love you."

When Maria got to ICU, it was a beehive of activity. Nurses were coming in and out to check monitors, change bandages, and administer medications, and a few doctors were visiting patients on their rounds. Walking into her mother's room, Maria noticed tubing had been placed in her mouth, and a tube from her catheter looked like it had blood in it. Maria shuddered as a sense of the seriousness of Carmella's condition struck her. It didn't look like she was going to regain consciousness anytime soon.

Times with her mother when she was growing up started to flash through Maria's mind. She saw her mother bringing a birthday cake to the table at a party when she turned eleven. Her mother was grinning from ear to ear. It was one of the happiest times she could recall. Then she remembered her mother driving her to high school and leaning over to kiss her before she got out of the car.

"Ms. D'Angelo?" The nurse's voice roused Maria from her daydream.

"Oh, yes," Maria said, somewhat embarrassed for her temporary detachment from the present. "I see she's got some new tubes. What are they for?"

"Dr. Harvey was in earlier and he was concerned about her breathing, so he ordered breathing tubes to be inserted." She pointed to a machine. "This machine gently pumps air into her lungs and makes sure her breathing is regular."

"That doesn't sound good," Maria said.

"No, we don't use tubes unless there is a real problem with breathing."

"How long do you think she'll need the tubes?"

"You need to ask the doctor that question. But if she regains consciousness, we may take the tubes out to see how she does on her own." The nurse looked at the monitor on the computer she had wheeled in on a stand. "I see Dr. Harvey has ordered another brain scan and a chest x-ray. I'm sure he'll talk to you after she gets those done."

"Is there anything else you can tell me about her condition?" Maria asked.

"That's about it. As I said, the doctor will talk to you when he comes back."

"But if he was just here, when will he be back?"

"You never know with these docs. They have busy schedules. But I'd guess it will be around the noon hour," the nurse said as she disconnected the catheter bag and replaced it with a fresh one.

CHAPTER 9

Gabe had been out nearly three hours, having run down to Maple Grove and back. He had paid close attention to his surroundings and felt confident no one was following him, so near the end of his run, he stopped in a little coffee shop for a latte and a muffin to replenish his energy. He felt a little tired, but refreshed. Then he walked the last quarter mile back to the condo. He approached the rear entrance to the building, which had a stairway to the basement and another door leading to the small open area just inside the front entrance. He walked through the front, took the little stairway to the second floor, and approached his door. It wasn't locked.

"Andy?" Gabe shouted. But there was only silence.

Gabe opened the door and saw the place had been ransacked. Drawers were open and thrown on the floor, the small bookshelf was knocked over, and cushions were thrown from the sofa and chairs. He walked into the kitchen.

"No!" he screamed when he saw the gory mess. Andy had been duct-taped to a kitchen chair toppled over with him in it. Andy's face was full of bloody wounds and cuts from being beaten. A single bullet wound to the forehead had no doubt caused him to fall backward. Gabe knew instinctively this was the work of Raph and his hench-men. But how had they found him? Were they outside waiting for him now? They must have found Andy working on the sink, tied him up, and beaten him for any information about Gabe and what was in the apartment. Andy wouldn't have known much, and the hit squad ran out of patience after ransacking the place.

Suddenly, it dawned on Gabe that he had not been to the bedroom. He drew his pistol from the holster under his shirt and went around the corner to the bedroom, clasping the pistol with both hands in front of him. He backed up and slowly eased in front of the door, one step at a time. The room appeared to be clear. Gabe checked under the bed and in the closets. The few clothes he had brought were off the hangers and on the floor along with the dresser drawers and his bedding. Next, he checked the bathroom. The shower curtain was already pulled open and the room was empty. As far as Gabe could tell, nothing was missing because he had left nothing of value. It was time to leave. If his pursuers weren't still in the area, they'd be back soon. Gabe quickly gathered up some toiletries from the floor into his shaving kit and left, keeping his gun low but still in his hand as he navigated the stairs.

The small lobby was empty. He glanced out the front door; nothing seemed unusual. Gabe hurried toward the rear of the building and the stairs to the basement, then stepped down cautiously, not knowing if anyone was there. In the basement, there were small storage lockers for each unit behind woven wire screens. Gabe unlocked his unit's space and removed a blanket that was thrown over a small duffle bag and a larger backpack containing essentials he would need in a quick getaway. He grabbed them and left through the rear door. There was no question of taking the car; the D'Angelos surely had identified it and put a tracker on it. Even if Gabe could remove it, they knew the make and model. Gabe thought he heard sirens as he walked briskly toward the rear entrance of the development.

CHAPTER 10

Maria sat alone in the ICU by her mother's bed; the rhythmic sounds of the breathing machine nearly caused her to doze off. Raph was gone for a few hours, and Rose had left to pick up Tessa from school. It was a half day at Tessa's school, and Rose would come back after she got a babysitter lined up since Rose and Raph had decided they didn't want Tessa to see her grandmother in her current condition.

"Ms. D'Angelo?" A voice roused Maria out of her daze. It was Dr. Harvey.

"Yes. Sorry, I must have zoned out for a minute."

"I got the results back from your mother's scan and chest x-ray and I'm sorry, but the news isn't good," the doctor said with a soft voice.

"Really, what's wrong?"

"The scan shows some further ischemic activity, with some hemorrhaging in the brain, and the x-ray shows your mother has significant fluid in her lungs. I'm afraid the prognosis isn't promising."

"I don't understand," Maria said. "Could you put that more simply?"

"The stroke is worse than we thought, possibly due to one or more additional strokes. This means there is very likely significant damage to your mother's brain, making it unlikely she will recover.

The fluid in the lungs probably indicates pneumonia from her weakened condition."

"So what do we do now?"

"There's not much we can do. If we disconnect the breathing tube, your mother's heart will probably slow until it stops beating. Again, I'm so sorry," the doctor said with a sad expression on his face. "Is your family coming back soon?"

"I expect my sister-in-law will be back soon. We can call my brother and get him to come back as well."

"When you're all together, have the nurse page me and I'll come talk to you. I expect to be here most of the afternoon."

"Okay, thank you."

"I believe your mother has an advance directive on file in my office. I'll call and get it sent over."

As soon as the doctor left, Maria took her phone out of her purse and dialed Brian's number. With any luck, he'd still be on his lunch hour.

The call went to voicemail. "Brian, please call me," she said with desperation in her voice. "Brian, I really need you right now. I don't know why you don't want to talk to me, but I'm sorry if it was something I did. I'm at the hospital with my mother and it's not going well. So … goodbye. I hope you'll call me soon." Maria put the phone down on the end table beside her seat. She sighed and looked upward, shaking her head.

Then, remembering what the doctor said, she picked up her phone again and dialed Raph's number. It went right to voicemail as well. "Raph. It's Maria. The doctor was just here and he wants to speak to all of us. Mother still has her breathing tube in and the doctor thinks she has pneumonia. Could you come by as soon as possible? Bring Rose. She's home meeting the babysitter for Tessa. Please come quickly."

CHAPTER 11

Raph was driving home from the clubhouse, where he and his captains conducted most of their business. It was about a forty-five minute drive back to Chestnut Hill, longer in rush hour. Phil called to explain the situation in Warminster.

"How the hell did he get away?" Raph roared. "I thought he was in the condo and his car was parked out front. You told me he hadn't moved it all night."

"That's right. He must have gone out for a walk or something."

"So why didn't you just wait for him? He couldn't have gone far."

"Well, there was another complication," Phil said. "The door wasn't locked, and when we went in, there was a guy fixing the sink."

"Great. Did he know where Gabe went?"

"He reached into his pocket and we both drew on him. He knew we had him. Then we tied him to a chair and, uh, questioned him," Phil said.

"So what did he tell you?"

"Nothing. Either he didn't know or he wouldn't tell us. I really don't think he knew anything. We got pretty rough with him."

"So now there's a plumber who's gonna call the police and give a description?"

"No. We didn't leave him as a witness," Phil said.

"So you went to whack Rossi, you killed a plumber, and Rossi got away? You really screwed this one up. I hope you got out of there, 'cause somebody may have called it in."

"Yeah. We wiped the place down and got out. We're parked at a Starbucks five minutes away. Do you want us to go back there?"

"No, somebody may have seen your car. Might have seen you too."

"We can drive by the complex and see if the cops are there. No one will notice this car."

"All right, you do that," Raph said, sounding disgusted. "Stick around the area a while and I'll call you back. Maybe you'll spot Rossi. And make sure somebody is watching the GPS in case he comes for his car."

Raph threw the phone down and shook his head in disgust. "What a shit show," he said out loud. "We had him, and now we'll have to start from scratch."

✦　✦　✦

Betty Morgan sat in her second-floor apartment staring out the window. Her little white poodle, Snowball, stood barking at her, letting her know it was feeding time. "Just wait a minute, Snowball. I think I need to call the police," she said as she picked up the old-style landline phone on the table beside her. She didn't want to be a busybody, but after she thought about what she had seen and heard, she decided to make the call. After all, she lived alone and was worried about the break-ins she had heard about from time to time. Had she just witnessed one, she wondered? She dialed nine-one-one.

"What is your name, ma'am, and where do you live?" the operator asked.

"Yes, officer, my name is Betty Morgan. I live in The Forest in Warminster, unit three two zero two. I had my window open earlier and I heard the worst screaming coming from the building across from me. That would be building number four where the noise was coming from. It must have gone on for fifteen minutes."

"Was it a man's or a woman's voice?" the operator asked.

"I believe it was a man's voice, although the way they were shrieking, it was hard to tell."

"What happened when the screaming stopped?"

"I think I heard a pop sound and the screaming stopped. Then a couple minutes later, two men left the building and went to their car in the parking lot for my building. I thought it was odd that they parked here when they were in the building across the street. There are open spaces over there," Betty said.

"Did you get a look at the two men?"

"Not really. They were wearing caps and sunglasses. I think one was older, maybe in his fifties and the other one looked younger."

"Ma'am, please stay in your apartment and we'll send a policeman over. He'll stop at your apartment, and you can point out to him where you heard the screams coming from."

♦　♦　♦

Less than a half hour after Betty Morgan phoned the police, there were four Warminster Township Police vehicles parked in front of what had been Gabe's building, and unit 4201 was taped off as a crime scene. A fifth car pulled up and stopped. It was Detective Dan Ritinski, a tall, muscular man with a graying crewcut.

"So, what have we got here?" the detective asked, looking at Sergeant Scott Anderson, the senior police officer present.

"I was first on the scene," Anderson said. "The neighbor across the street heard some loud screaming that went on for ten minutes or so. She said it stopped after she heard a pop sound. I went to her apartment and she said the screaming came from this building. She saw two men leave soon afterward but didn't get a good look at their faces. The door of this unit was ajar, and when I entered, I found what's now in front of us."

"Any ID of the victim?" Ritinski asked.

"Negative on that. The vic's wallet is missing. This might have been a robbery gone bad based on the place being totally ransacked."

The detective slipped on a pair of latex gloves and bent over with a small flashlight to inspect the body. "Did anyone look in that toolbox?" When no one answered, Ritinski carefully probed the inside of the box. "Looks like he was doing some plumbing." Ritinski picked up a Home Depot bag containing a few PVC pipe fittings, pulled out a receipt, and placed it in a plastic evidence bag. "We should be able to get an ID from this receipt since a credit card was used." Ritinski continued to inspect the body. "Not much question about what killed the victim," he said. "I'd like to know more about the other injuries. Is the coroner on the way?"

"They have a van coming." Anderson said.

The detective checked out the bedroom, and Anderson followed close behind. "I don't think this was a robbery," Ritinski said. "A drug deal, maybe. It looks like this unit was vacant. The intruder might have come here and stumbled on someone working on the plumbing from the looks of things. But then why tie the guy up, beat him so badly, and shoot him?" he asked, as if thinking out loud. He took a picture of the Home Depot receipt with his phone and sent it back to his office.

"I want you guys to get right on canvassing the neighbors to see if anyone besides the witness who called this in saw anything. What about prints?" the detective asked.

"Looks like the place was wiped clean," Anderson said. "But we got some partials on two coffee cups in the sink."

"That's interesting. Maybe our victim served coffee to the intruder. Or maybe someone else was here with the victim. Let's run those prints right away. Any shell casings?"

"Nope. Must have been picked up. But check out the hole in the wall behind where the victim was sitting. It's hard to see with the blood splatter."

Ritinski shined his light on the blood splatter on the wall, then took out his pen knife to see if he could dig a bullet out. "The bullet's too deep for me to pry out. Make sure the techs get it." Ritinski's phone rang. "Oh yeah? That's interesting. Can you text me an address?" He listened for another minute, then hung up.

"They got an ID from the receipt. Andrew Carr, lives in Hatboro. Not only that, he's got a pretty long sheet. Mostly arrests related to bookmaking. Maybe he owed the wrong guy money. Let's get the prints processed as soon as we can," Ritinski added as he made his way to the door.

Chapter 12

"I know this is an extremely difficult time for you," Dr. Harvey said as Maria, Rose, and Raph listened with rapt attention.

"So you're telling us there's really no hope for our mother?" Raph asked.

"What I'm saying is her prognosis isn't good. She isn't able to breathe without the respirator right now. She might make it a few more days, or she might not make it through the night."

"Is there a chance she could show some improvement by tomorrow?" Maria asked hopefully, wiping tears from her eyes.

"It's possible, but unlikely," Dr. Harvey said. "Her advance directive says she doesn't want to be kept alive by artificial means if there's no likelihood of recovery."

"So, does that mean we need to take her breathing tube out?" Raph asked.

"Not right away. We have some flexibility. My suggestion is that we get together in the morning and I can update you on her condition. If she isn't showing any improvement, you all can consider having us remove the breathing tube."

"How long can we keep her on the machine?" Rose asked.

"In about two or three days, the hospital will review her case and have a committee of three doctors examine her and review her chart.

If they all think she's not going to recover, the hospital will enforce her advance directive and remove the breathing tube. It usually doesn't go that far with a patient at your mother's age and in her condition. If the patient doesn't die on her own first, the families usually follow the directive before the hospital gets involved.

"Okay, I think we understand. Thank you, Doctor. We'll discuss it with you tomorrow morning. Is that okay with you two?" Raph asked, looking at Maria and Rose. They nodded yes.

"I've got to go and take care of some things," Raph said. "I can come back tonight."

"I'd like to go to Mother's condo. I want her to have her rosary when the time comes," Maria said in a broken voice.

"That's very sweet of you, Maria. I think I'll just stay here and sit with her," Rose said, wiping away her own tears.

"Does Henry know we probably won't need him anymore?" Maria asked.

"I don't know. If you want, you can have him call me. I'll make sure he's well taken care of," Raph said.

◆　◆　◆

As Maria pulled out of the hospital, she heard a phone in her purse ring. It wasn't her regular phone, but the one Gabe had given her. She really didn't want to talk to Gabe right now. After about ten rings, the phone went quiet. Then, a few minutes later it started ringing again. She pulled off the road into a gas station lot and answered the phone.

"Gabe?"

"Thanks for taking my call. How is your mother?"

"Not good. She's on a breathing machine and the doctor is talking to us about taking her off of it. He tried to sugar coat it a little, but he doesn't think she's going to recover."

"I'm really sorry to hear that. I knew your mother and considered her a good friend, at least before all the stuff began in court."

"Thank you, Gabe."

"But the reason I called is that I'm really in a bad situation. Your brother has a contract out on my life."

"What?" Maria shrieked. She had already heard from Rose that Gabe was in danger but it hadn't sunk in that Raph would actually murder him.

"His people already made one attempt," Raph said.

"I can't believe it," Maria said, gasping. "Maybe there's something I can do. Maybe I can plead with him! After all, you saved my life once. That should count for something with Raph," Maria said.

"I doubt that will do any good. A man was killed this morning who was in the condo where I was staying. I think I was the intended victim."

"Oh my gosh, no! Are you sure?"

"Yes. It was a guy I knew from way back who loaned me the place. He was there fixing the sink and I went out for a run. When I came back, he was dead."

"And you think Raph is behind this?"

"Yes, I'm sure of it."

"I can't believe this. My mother is dying, they're asking us to take her off life support, and this is what my brother is doing?"

"Raph can't let go of the fact that I testified against your father. It's an old rule in families like this that you don't testify against them." Gabe paused. "I'm sorry, I know you're not a part of this, but it's true."

"Gabe, as I said before, why not get in your car and drive as far away from here as you can?"

"I tried witness protection, but I just don't want to be away from here. This has been my home all my life. My friends, what's left of my family, my schools—they're all in this area. And even if I did decide to leave town, I can't just go. It would take some planning."

"So what are you going to do?"

"I figure that if I can beat these threats, I can find a way to settle in here."

"How are you going to do that, Gabe? If what you say is true, do you really think Raph is going to back down?"

"I've got some ideas on that, but I can't go into details," Gabe said as he thought about the evidence he had implicating Raph.

"You're not going to kill Raph, are you?" Maria asked.

"No, I don't think that will be necessary."

"Gabe, we need to stop the violence. One thing my father did right was to try to get his business away from that. If you promise me you won't do anything violent or illegal, I'll help you if I can. Is there anything I can do?"

"Do you know of anywhere I could stay for a few days? I can't go back to my dead friend's condo. You helped me once before, and I hate to ask you again, but I'm out of options."

Maria thought for a moment. "Can you meet me somewhere?"

"Yeah. I can take an Uber," Gabe said.

"Let me give you an address. I'll be there in a few minutes. I'll tell the attendant in the lobby that I'm expecting you."

◆　◆　◆

As Gabe approached York Road, he saw a Starbucks. He went around the back of the Jiffy Lube next door. Nearing the coffee shop, he carefully concealed himself behind cars in the parking lot until he could get to a place where he could see the inside. He took a small pair of binoculars out of his backpack. There was a bit of glare on the shop's window, but he could make out Phil Morino and Denny Delvato drinking a late morning latte. Gabe had a hunch that Phil was likely involved in the killing, and his hunch panned out. Why else would they be in the area? Gabe also knew Morino was addicted to coffee, especially from Starbucks, so he figured Phil and whoever was helping him might be there cooling their heels after their visit to the condo.

Gabe reached in his pocket and felt the shell casing he had taken from the apartment and put in a little plastic bag. It was sloppy work on their part to leave it. *They must have left in a big hurry,* he thought.

Gabe maneuvered his way back to the Jiffy Lube and followed an alley along the back side of several businesses until he reached a small strip mall containing a beauty salon, a real estate agency, and a bagel shop. The parking lot was almost full, so it was an easy place to blend in. He ducked into the bagel shop and requested an Uber on his phone using an alias and credit card he had maintained during his time in witness protection. The Uber took about six minutes to arrive. Gabe slipped into the back seat of of a Hyundai Santa Fe, threw his bags to the side, and laid his head back against the seat for what he expected to be a peaceful forty-five-minute ride. Gabe didn't usually talk to Uber drivers. In fact, he rarely used Uber, and he didn't feel like talking now.

"You see all the police cars down the street?" the driver asked. He was a stout middle-aged man with short reddish hair and spoke with the accent of someone who grew up in working-class Philadelphia.

"No. Where are they?"

"They're back in that condo complex around the corner. Heard there was a shooting or something back there. Did you hear anything about it?"

"No."

"My brother-in-law is on the police force here. I get a lot of the inside scoop."

"You don't say," Gabe said.

"A murder is pretty unusual. Not much violent crime around here. Maybe a few break-ins, but no murders. You from around here?"

"The city."

The driver's connection to the police department made Gabe even more reluctant to speak. Gabe pulled his cap down low and pretended to look down to study his phone. There was no point in giving this guy a good look at his face.

"Oh, so you're used to crime," the driver said. "Yeah, I know some parts of the city are safe, mostly where the rich people live. But some other parts you couldn't pay me to go into. I don't do pickups in a lot of areas. The area you're headed to is pretty safe, though. You live in Chestnut Hill?"

"No. Just visiting a friend."

"Lots of rich people there. I see you're going to Germantown Avenue. Pretty nice place."

Gabe didn't answer, so the driver kept talking. "They say the leader of the mafia used to live in Chestnut Hill. A few years ago, they finally nailed him and he's in prison. Yeah, those are some guys I wouldn't want to tangle with."

"Neither would I," Gabe replied.

CHAPTER 13

Detective Ritinski sat at his desk writing up his report on the crime scene at the apartment complex. He started to create a "murder book," a notebook of all the significant developments in the case, including witness statements, notes, and a catalog of the physical evidence. The murder book would serve as his bible while investigating and hopefully solving the case. In his nineteen years as a detective on the force, he had only made three other murder books; two of the cases had been solved, the third remained unsolved. The detective heard someone approaching his desk. When he looked up, it was Sergeant Anderson.

"Did you submit the prints to the lab?" Ritinski asked.

"Yeah, over an hour ago. I sent the victim's prints too and put a rush on it.

"You find anything more about the victim?" the detective asked.

"Yeah. He lives in a townhouse in Hatboro and he actually owns the unit where we found the victim," Anderson said.

"What was he, a landlord?" the detective asked.

"Looks that way. A bookmaker and a landlord. Sounds like he was an enterprising guy," Anderson said.

"And a plumber on top of all that," Ritinski said. "How about the neighbors? Anybody see anything?"

"Other than the woman who called, we're coming up empty. Most of the neighbors were at work. One guy in the same building on the ground floor works from home. He thought he heard something, but he was on the computer and had earbuds in his ears," Anderson said. "Oh, I almost forgot. One guy said he saw someone deliver a pizza last night. He thought it was strange that the guy parked by Building Three, walked right past Building Four, and went to the next building. He didn't see the car the delivery guy came in, though."

"I assume there was no video footage?" the detective asked.

"Nope. There's a camera at the entrance but it wasn't working."

"Just our luck. A camera might have clinched the case for us."

A woman approached the two officers from the hallway leading to the front reception. "Sarge, I buzzed your desk but you didn't answer. You've got a call from the lab. They said it's urgent."

"That was quick," Ritinski said.

Sergeant Anderson disappeared around the corner for about ten minutes while Detective Ritinski continued to work on his book. When Anderson returned, there was a big grin on his face.

"Dan, wait until you hear this!"

Chapter 14

Gabe was impressed with the elegant old building where the Uber dropped him off. He was especially glad to get away from the overly chatty driver. Gabe felt sure he had not given the driver a good enough look at his face to give a description. A doorman stood under a canopy and opened the front door and Gabe entered a lobby with rich hardwood paneling, a marble checkered floor, and a large desk behind which another man in uniform stood. The man had been reading some sheets of paper but looked up when Gabe approached, still wearing his sunglasses and a baseball cap pulled low.

"Are you here to see Ms. D'Angelo?" the man asked.

"Yes I am."

"Okay, Mr. Roth, please just sign our guest log and I'll send you right up."

Gabe and Maria had agreed he would use the name "Roth" while visiting the building. Gabe glanced around quickly and didn't see any cameras, then took the elevator to the second floor and found his way to unit 202. After he rang the old-style buzzer, Maria opened the door. She stood aside and Gabe entered an expansive foyer leading to a living room with hardwood floors, an oriental rug, and a fireplace. In the corner stood a grand piano.

"Come in, Gabe. I don't have much time," Maria said.

"Thanks again for helping me. This is a beautiful place. Is it yours?"

"No. It's my mother's." Maria paused and took a breath, as if thinking about her mother. "She moved out of the house when my father went to prison. I think it's safe for you to stay here a few days. Let me just finish something and I'll show you around."

Maria turned to a dining area off the living room. She had some papers, some beads, and a Bible she was packing into a little canvas bag.

"How is your mother doing? I assume she's in the hospital for a while?" Gabe asked.

"She's not doing well," Maria said. She put her arm on the table, leaned on it, and brushed her hair out of her face. There was a tear on her cheek. "She's on a breathing machine, and we're probably going to take her off of it tomorrow, so she won't be coming back here."

"I'm so sorry, Maria," Gabe said, gently touching her shoulder. "I know you're under a lot of stress right now, but I want you to know how much I appreciate your help. I wouldn't keep bothering you with my problems if I wasn't so desperate," he said. "But what about your brother? Doesn't he come here?"

"He hardly came here when my mother was living here. He always had her picked up and brought to the house, and I don't think he has any interest in coming around now. He doesn't need her furniture or anything. But even if he comes, you'll still be safe. Let me show you."

Maria walked Gabe around the corner to a hallway. The first door led to a bedroom that was clearly Carmella's. There was a wheelchair sitting next to the bed and a narrow table on wheels that could be swung around to serve someone in the bed. The second bedroom appeared to be a smaller guest bedroom with a futon and some bookshelves and a large window looking down on a flower garden. At the end of the hallway was a closed door. Maria took out a key and unlocked it. It led to a small sitting room and a third bedroom equipped with a bed, a dresser with a large mirror, and a walk-in closet. There was a small computer table and chairs, some file cabinets, and a television attached to the wall on one side.

"This is where Henry stayed when he was taking care of Mother. He's moved out now and won't be coming back, at least not to stay," Maria explained. "Henry was her caregiver. I really don't think Raph will show up, but look," she said, walking to a large glass door that led to a small balcony. She opened the door to provide a better view. To the right was a stairway leading to the rear of the building. "This is a fire escape. You can use it if you need to leave in a hurry and can't go out the front.

"There's food and supplies in the kitchen. Just be careful not to leave a mess or it will look suspicious if someone does show up. The man at reception goes off duty at five and a new guy comes in for the evening. There will be people coming and going, so the night receptionist won't know you're here."

"Thank you, Maria. You are a saint."

"I'm anything but a saint. But you saved me three years ago, and you got hurt badly protecting me. So I owe you."

"You don't owe me anything, Maria. Will you be back?"

"I'll try to come back to check on you, but I'm not sure when in view of my mother's condition. I'll call or text to let you know I'm coming. You can text me if something happens here, or if you need anything."

Gabe gave her a quick hug. "Thanks again for all this."

CHAPTER 15

Detective Ritinski felt annoyed at the amount of time he had to spend on hold when he tried to telephone the FBI field office in Philadelphia. After several false starts and being routed to the wrong person, he was connected to Special Agent Perez.

"Detective Ritinski, what can I do for you?" she asked.

"We're investigating a murder at an apartment building in Warminster. The victim was the owner of the unit and was working on some plumbing when an intruder entered. He was tied to a chair, beaten, and shot in the head."

"Yes, I heard a report about that on the news. I assume you've identified the victim?"

"Yes, it was a guy named Andrew Carr. He ran a bookmaking operation in the area. He was apparently renting out the apartment because he lives at another address in Hatboro. He's got a significant arrest record although he hasn't done any hard time."

"So how does this involve the FBI?" Agent Perez asked.

"We got partial prints on two coffee cups left in the sink. One of the prints was Carr's and the other one was someone who was flagged in the report as being in witness protection. I just faxed the report over to you."

"Okay, just bear with me," she said as she tried to pull up the fax. "Okay, I see it. Yes, this is very interesting. I'm pretty sure the unnamed subject is someone we're looking for."

"We've got a murder to investigate, so if there's anything you can share with us, that would be very helpful. We can share information with you as well."

"Yes, we can do that."

"It says in the report the subject was named Randy Sherman and he was residing out of state. How is it that he's in our area?"

"I can only share limited information right now, but the subject is from Philly and he's got connections with organized crime. He's also got a history of violence, so I would urge caution. Because he was in witness protection, Randy Sherman is not his real name, which he would have been known by when he lived in the area."

"Looks like this guy is now our number-one suspect in the murder. I'm thinking the subject may have come to collect a debt, or maybe settle a score from the past," Ritinski said.

"Did you guys get a description or any other forensic evidence?"

"No, other than we've got two vehicles in the lot. One is clearly Carr's and the other may have belonged to our suspect. He must have left in a hurry if he abandoned his car."

"Could be," Agent Perez said.

"Any way we could get some info on the suspect, like his real name, a description, or photos?"

"I think we can probably do that, but I need to run this by my superiors. Before releasing information, we also need to send a team out to look at the crime scene. Are the vehicles still there?"

"Yeah. Let me know when you're coming. We've got the key to Carr's vehicle but we don't have keys to the one that may have belonged to the suspect."

"Will do. If you were planning a press conference or press release, could you hold off until you hear from me? I'll do my best to get back to you tonight."

"Sure thing," Ritinski said.

◆　◆　◆

Agent Perez called Agent McIntyre right after speaking to Ritinski.

"Anything on the CCTV searches?" she asked.

"We got a sighting of him leaving a bar on Lombard Street last week. He seemed to be in a hurry, and we don't have the clearest view of his face. He seems to have disappeared into the woodwork after that, but at least it confirms he's in the area."

"Well, I just got a report from a detective in Warminster, up near Maple Grove, and they've got fingerprint evidence that places Rossi at a murder scene there."

"No kidding!" McIntyre said with a gasp. "That certainly thickens the plot."

"It sure does," she said. "We need to get a forensics team up there. It looks like Rossi may have left his car there as well."

"If he left his car there, he may have left on foot and could still be nearby. I'll get some agents to patrol the area."

"I'll text you the address of the crime scene and the contact info for the local detective," she said.

CHAPTER 16

Raph stood by the bed with a blank stare on his face as a medical technician unhooked the tube from the breathing machine. Maria and Rose stood on either side of him, both wiping tears from their eyes. After turning off the the machine, the technician removed the tape that was holding the breathing tube in place and gently grasped where the tube extended into Carmella's mouth, giving it a little twist until she could slide it out.

Maria clutched her own rosary beads and tearfully whispered "Hail Mary, Mother of God, blessed art thou among women and blessed is the fruit of thy womb, Jesus ..."

Rose stared intently at the small computer screen that showed her mother-in-law's vitals. The reading for breaths per minute quickly dropped from sixteen to fourteen, and her pulse dropped from seventy-five beats to sixty. Maria wondered how long this would go on now that her mother had no help breathing. Would she hang on for hours?

An alarm beeped loudly as her breaths per minute dropped to twelve, then to eleven. The technician quickly pressed some buttons to disable the alarms so her patient could slip away quietly. The monitor showed Carmella's breaths dropping to nine per minute, then eight. Her heartbeat dropped to forty-nine, then forty-one, then thirty-eight. Another alarm sounded.

The technician apologized. "I'm sorry, these machines have a mind of their own." She hit another button to mute the alarm.

The various numbers on the screen continued to drop as the three watched. In a few moments the heartrate flat-lined, and it was over, just like that. A nurse they had not seen came up behind them and said "Nine forty-nine a.m." The tech looked at her and nodded as the nurse made a notation on her clipboard, then expertly disconnected the remainder of the tubes and monitoring equipment, pulled out the IV line, and removed the tape.

"We'll leave you alone with her for a bit. Take your time. When you're done, we'll move your mother to another location," the nurse said.

Rose began to wail. Maria hugged Rose as Raph stood staring stoically at his mother's body.

"Raph, are you heading home now?" Maria asked.

"I'm not sure. I'll be there soon, but there are some things I need to take care of."

"Why don't I take Rose home, and we'll see you there soon," Maria said.

"Okay, I need to try to get a message to Dad. We'll probably get some visitors later today at the house."

Maria knew the visitors would consist primarily of Gus Nasuti and some of Raph's mafia captains. She didn't relish being there for that gathering, but she knew Rose shouldn't be alone right now.

Maria felt numb. She wondered why she didn't feel the strong emotions Rose did. Maybe it was because over the past several days she had been stressed out over her mother being in the ICU and the meetings with Doctor Harvey. Plus there was the matter of Gabe hiding at her mother's condo, and the fact that he was in mortal danger because of her own brother. No doubt Raph had put the word out for all soldiers to be on the lookout for Gabriel Rossi. On top of all that, she hadn't heard from Brian and knew there was something seriously wrong with their relationship.

She, Raph, and Rose had a meeting scheduled with a funeral director the next day to go over the arrangements. Maria wanted her mother to have the service she deserved, but she was anxious to get it over with so life could go back to normal—or near normal. It was hard for her to consider her life normal while she was protecting Gabe from Raph. Maria hoped that situation could be resolved soon, so Gabe would be free to leave and start a new life. She resolved to speak to Raph about this as soon as possible.

◆　◆　◆

Raph entered the lobby of his mother's condo building on Germantown Avenue in Chestnut Hill.

"Lewis," Raph said to the man behind the desk. "Any mail?"

"Good morning Mr. D'Angelo. Yes, there are some items here. Henry usually picks up the mail, but I haven't seen him since your mother was taken to the hospital. By the way, how is Carmella? Is she doing better?"

"She passed away," Raph said, pursing his lips.

"Oh, I'm so sorry to hear that. I've only known her since she moved in about three years ago, but she was a wonderful woman." Lewis produced a stack of mail bound together with a rubber band. "If there's anything I can do, please let me know."

"Thank you, Lewis. Henry's moved out, so I'll stop by every few days to check on the mail. If you need to reach me, you've got my number."

"Of course. Your sister came into the condo the other day. Please give her my condolences as well," Lewis said.

"Yeah, she had to pick up some things."

"I didn't know the man who came to see her. A Mr. Roth, I believe," he said. Raph had an informal arrangement with Lewis to keep an eye on those coming and going from the unit.

"Was Mr. Roth there very long?" Raph asked.

"I'm not sure. It was near the end of my shift, but I didn't see anyone leave before I left."

"I'm drawing a blank on Mr. Roth. What did he look like?" Raph asked.

"He was a tall fellow, maybe about six feet tall. He was wearing a baseball cap and sunglasses, so I couldn't get a good look. He did sign in, though."

Was this Gabe? "Let me see the sign-in log for that day. Maybe that will jog my memory." Sure enough, someone named "Roth" had signed in at four, about fifteen minutes after Maria signed in. It had to be Gabe. Maria had signed out around four thirty.

"I don't see a sign-out for this Mr. Roth," Raph said.

"Oh, that's not unusual. People forget they're supposed to sign out, and with so many people coming and going, we don't always notice the guests leaving," Lewis said.

"Thanks." Raph was now almost sure it was Gabe who came to visit Maria. Maybe he was there right now. He had to give Maria credit for her bold plan to hide Gabe in their own mother's condo. Right now, however, he didn't want to go up to the unit. Knowing Gabe, he would be armed and ready for any unfriendly visitors, and Raph didn't want a hit to occur in his mother's residence. He stepped outside and made a phone call to Phil Morino.

"Phil," Raph said.

Before he could go further, Phil said, "Raph, I'm really sorry about your mother. Gus filled me in."

"Thanks, but I might have some big news. I think I found Gabe, and I need your help."

"Oh yeah? Where is he?"

"He's in my mother's condo. It's the Fairmount on Germantown Avenue."

"No shit! How did he get there?"

"My guess is Maria offered it to him as a place to cool his heels for a while."

"You want a team to come over and finish the job?"

"Not in my mother's condo. That's the least I can do to show her some respect. She's not even buried yet. Send a couple guys over here right away to watch the entrance. Make sure they're guys who remember what Gabe looks like. If he's in there, we've got him trapped, and we can take him if he tries to leave. I'll stay till our guys get here. We're not going to let him get away this time."

"Sure thing, boss," Phil said.

◆　◆　◆

About a half hour later, the team arrived at the Fairmount—Frankie Lombardo and Dom Tartaglia—two loyal soldiers who listened to directions and could be trusted to conduct the stakeout effectively. Raph explained the situation to them and ordered one to stay out front and the other to watch the back in case Gabe found a service elevator. Raph walked around the building and saw the shades were drawn in his mother's condo. This reinforced his suspicions since his mother always kept them open.

"If he comes out, let us know right away and tail him. Don't let him out of your sight. Another crew will handle the hit, so don't try and take him yourselves. And if my sister Maria comes, make sure she doesn't get hurt. If anything happens to her, I'll hold you guys responsible," Raph said.

After setting up the stakeout, Raph left for the clubhouse, where he planned to hold a meeting with his captains. When he arrived, several of them were already seated in the room where Raph usually held meetings. It was a no-frills space with a large table and some smaller tables off to the side, snacks and various alcoholic beverages, and a big screen television with some comfortable chairs in front of it. The captains stood when Raph walked in.

"Sorry boss about your mother," said Ange Mancini, one of Raph's top captains.

"Thanks Ange. We're having a get-together at my house tonight. I hope you're all able to come."

Various members of the group nodded. When Phil Morino and Tony Marianni walked in, Raph looked up with a scowl on his face. He had not forgotten that Phil had let Gabe get away and killed a plumber instead. Raph suspected Phil had not gotten to the scene as early as he had let on, despite his assurances that he'd be there.

"Who's at the stakeout in Chestnut Hill?" Raph asked, looking at Phil.

"We got Frankie and Dom up there," Phil said.

"Any word from them?" Raph asked.

"No. Nothing's happened. I got them phoning me every half hour."

Just then, Raph's phone buzzed. It was Gus Nasuti. "Where the hell are you?"

"I'll be there in five minutes, but turn on the news," Gus said.

The group got up and moved to the furniture in front of the television as Raph hit the "On" button on the controller.

The news announcer began to speak as the music introducing the program faded. "This is Jim Garner from Action News reporting on a murder investigation in Warminster Township, Montgomery County. In this small town that rarely sees violence, what appeared at first glance to be a break-in gone wrong has caught the attention not only of the local authorities but also the FBI. This morning, a local landlord was found murdered in an apartment, where he was doing some work. The police are looking for Gabriel Rossi, an associate of former Philadelphia mob boss Michael D'Angelo. D'Angelo is serving a twenty-five-year sentence in a federal penitentiary in Texas. Rossi testified against Michael D'Angelo at his trial three years ago and is believed to have left the federal witness protection program. Sources in the local police force have confirmed Rossi was at the scene shortly before the killing."

"Now that's what I call serendipity," Raph said.

"Seren what?" Charlie Beans asked. Charlie was an older member of the team.

"Look it up you moron," Raph said. "It means we got lucky. Phil and Denny went to that apartment to do a hit on Rossi because we knew he was staying there. But they killed the wrong guy. Now the cops think Rossi did it and are searching for him."

"Why do they think Rossi did it? I mean, how do the cops even know he was there?" Rudi, one of the captains asked.

"*We* knew he was there. Why couldn't the cops figure it out as well?" Phil asked.

"I got a source up there," Gus said. "He says that they found Rossi's fingerprint in the apartment. They ran it through the system and bingo. They got a convicted felon with a violent background at the crime scene. It looks like he was probably collecting a debt from this guy and the guy wouldn't pay."

"But if he gets arrested, we don't control the situation," Phil said.

"True, and the feds will probably let the state prosecute him for murder, and we all know he ain't gettin' out on bail since he already flew the coop once when he left witness protection."

"What if they can't make a case against him for murder?" Raph asked. "Just 'cause they put him at the crime scene doesn't prove he did it."

"We don't know what other evidence they have," Gus answered. "But even if they can't prove murder, Rossi's gonna end up back in the pen for breaking his parole. Either way, he's gonna be locked up, and we have contacts at most prisons to do the job."

"So, what are we gonna do?" Phil asked.

"For the moment, let's stay the course. I don't think the cops will find him if he's hiding in my mother's condo. If Rossi tries to leave, we'll nail him and that's the end of it. But if nothing happens in a day or so, I've got an idea," Raph said.

CHAPTER 17

Maria drove Rose home after discussing arrangements for her mother with hospital personnel. The numbness she had felt was being replaced by sorrow and grief. At the same time, she felt a sense of relief that the waiting was over. Another day of watching her mother languish in the intensive care unit would have been brutal. Rose asked Maria to stay with her while she spoke to Tessa about her grandmother's passing. Tessa let out a shriek and cried in her mother's arms for a few minutes, but her childish grief was short-lived. After a hug from Maria, she asked if she could go to her room and play a computer game.

"Are you okay, or do you want me to stay for a while?" Maria asked Rose after Tessa left.

"I'll be okay. I'm getting a headache and I need to lay down a bit," Rose said. "It would be great if you could be here tonight, though. Raph has some of his business partners coming to the house and he expects me to be here. There's going to be a lot of drinking, and I don't know if I can face it myself."

"Do you need help with the food, or setting up?" Maria asked.

"No. Raph's got a caterer lined up to handle everything. I just need some moral support. I don't want to be stuck having to talk to a bunch of middle-aged mafia men."

"I'm happy to come. We'll stick together, okay?"

"Maria, I don't know how to thank you enough. I'm pretty upset about Mom. You don't mind if I call her that, do you? Carmella was like the mother I never had."

"No. And thank you for being there for her through all this. I know you were always around when she needed you. Maybe tonight I can just be the sister you never had."

"I've always thought of you that way," Rose said as the two hugged and cried on each other's shoulders.

◆　◆　◆

As Maria drove home to get changed for the gathering, her phone rang. When she saw it was Brian calling, she picked up right away.

"Brian?"

"Yeah. Sorry I didn't return your calls or texts. Can you talk?"

"Yes. I'm driving home."

"Look, I'm really sorry about your mother and I'm sorry I wasn't there for you."

"Okay, but why? Why did you just stop talking to me?"

"I still want to be with you. It's just that when I saw you with that other guy, it was, well, a lot for me to bear."

"What are you talking about?" Maria asked.

"I came to the school. I was going to surprise you and take you to dinner. When I went around back, I saw you hugging some guy. Was that Gabe?"

"Oh my gosh, Brian! Yes, it was Gabe, but it's not what you think."

"What is he doing here? I thought he was in witness protection."

"He was, but he left and came back here. I guess he was homesick. Now he's in danger."

"I know you were close. It looked to me like he came back to pick up where you two left off."

"No. I mean yes, I was glad to see him and happy he's alive. But I promise you, there's nothing between us, at least not like you think."

"I saw the way he held you and stroked your back. It wasn't just a quick hug. What was I supposed to think?"

"You should think about our time together over the past three years," Maria said.

"I tried to do that, and I'm still trying to do that."

"But then you ghosted me. You weren't there when I needed you."

"I'm sorry for the way I reacted." Brian sighed. "I really feel relieved. I haven't been able to sleep since I saw you with him. I really do love you. Can I see you tonight?"

"I have to go to a wake at Raph's house. I really don't want to go, but I promised Rose I'd go so she's not alone with a bunch of his associates."

"Do you want me to come with you?" Brian asked.

"Thanks for offering, but it's probably better if you don't. I'll need to focus on Rose. Besides, if you knew all Raph was up to, you probably wouldn't want to come."

"Why, what's he doing?" Brian asked.

"I'll tell you more in person. Why don't we get together tomorrow?"

"I'd love that," Brian said.

CHAPTER 18

Maria arrived at Raph's house around seven. A catering truck was parked out front, and the employees were carrying trays inside. Maria didn't ring the doorbell since the front door was open.

"Rose?" she said as she stepped inside.

"I'm in here," Rose said from the kitchen. "I'm giving Tessa her dinner before I drop her off at a friend's house to stay overnight."

"Hi Aunt Maria," Tessa said. "Do you wanna take me to Julie's house?"

"Well, I'd be glad to, but it's up to your mother."

"Oh, could you take her?" Rose asked. "It's only about a ten-minute walk from here. That way I can keep an eye on the caterers to make sure they don't break anything."

Maria and Tessa left, walking hand in hand. The ten-minute walk turned into fifteen since Tessa kept dropping her overnight bag while trying to juggle the other boxes and bags containing Barbie dolls and video games. By the time they got there, Maria felt like a pack horse, carrying most of the stuff. Then she had to explain to Julie's mother the instructions Rose had told her to pass on. Forty minutes had passed by the time Maria got back, and the house was already filled with a pervasive bouquet of cigar smoke.

Maria made her way to Rose, who was straightening up the utensils and plates on a console near the food table. Almost immediately, Maria was cornered by a short, stocky man with thick, oily hair carrying a plate full of pasta and Italian sausages.

Rose made the introduction. "Maria, this is Rocky Messina. Rocky, this is Maria D'Angelo, Raph's sister."

"Oh yeah. You're the nun, or nun in training," Rocky said.

"Actually, I left the convent almost three years ago," Maria replied.

"I'm not surprised. You're too beautiful to be a nun. You'd make all the others look bad," Rocky said with a chuckle.

Rose took Maria by the arm and escorted her away as Rocky started to invade Maria's personal space.

"I thought *I* was here to protect *you*," Maria said to Rose with a smile.

"Believe me, you are protecting me. If you weren't here, they'd all be hitting on me," Rose said.

Gus Nasuti and Phil Morino approached with beer bottles in their hands. "You must be Michael's daughter, Maria. You're even more beautiful than I had heard," Phil said, putting his hand on Maria's shoulder.

Rose gently took Phil's arm and moved it away from Maria. "You guys better behave, or I'll have to tell Raph you're hitting on his sister!" Rose seemed to know exactly how to handle the members of this group.

"Hey now, no need to get uptight." Phil laughed. "Just tell Raph I was admiring his beautiful sister."

After several similar encounters, Rose led Maria to the kitchen, where two of the caterers were making hors d'oeuvres. Another one was washing dishes in the sink.

"Do they need help?" Maria asked.

"Whether they need it or not, let's give them a hand," Rose said. "It will hide us from the over-sexed capos out there."

Rose and Maria grabbed towels and began drying the dishes and stacking them on a table to be reused in the buffet. After about a half hour of helping in the kitchen, Rose and Maria grabbed bottles of champagne to make sure everyone drinking it had a full glass.

"I don't know about you, but I'm starved. There's some fantastic lasagna over here. Let's get some before they start putting the food away," Rose said.

The women took their plates to the sun porch, which had not previously been opened. They sat at a small table to enjoy their meals.

"How much longer is this going to go on?" Maria asked.

"It'll go pretty late into the night. They've still got a lot of booze to drink. I think Raph is going to give a little speech later, a tribute to Mom. I'm expected to be there for that, then afterwards I can go upstairs to bed."

"You'd better lock your door with this group around," Maria joked.

"Don't I know it."

As they were finishing up, Raph opened the glass doors leading to the porch and came in. "So this is where you've been hiding," he said with a smirk on his face.

"Yep, hiding in plain sight," Rose said.

"I need to talk to Maria for a sec," Raph said.

"I was just getting up to check on things in the kitchen," Rose said as she walked toward the doors.

"Are we all set for the mass next Saturday?" Raph asked Maria.

"I spoke to Father Pierce and we're booked at the church for ten in the morning, then refreshments in the church hall, and the graveside service at one."

"How about the funeral home?"

"We've got the space booked for the visitation on Friday. But we need to go and meet with the funeral director to finalize the casket selection and the details of the visitation," Maria said. "And we need to finalize the flowers and music."

"Look, Maria. You've done a great job so far and you're much better at these things than I am. I'm busy this week and I'm sure whatever you pick will be great. So why don't you just handle it? If you want Rose to help you, she will."

Maria took a deep breath and glared at Raph. "Maybe if you weren't so busy trying to kill Gabe, you'd have time to work on Mother's funeral," She wiped her lips with a cloth napkin and threw it down on the plate.

"What are you talking about?" Raph asked, his expression turning dark.

"You know very well what I'm talking about."

"So you're in contact with your old boyfriend. I wonder what Brian thinks about that."

"Don't avoid the real issue here. You're trying to kill the man who almost died saving my life."

"You need to stay away from Gabe. He's dangerous. Haven't you seen the news? He's wanted for murder," Raph said.

"What?"

"Yeah. Watch the news."

"So if he's wanted, why do you need to kill him?"

"He's the man who testified against our father. Why do you want to protect him?" Raph asked. "Do you think I have a choice in this? If Gabe had left town and stayed away, we wouldn't be having this conversation."

"Do you think Gabe had a choice? The FBI got his laptop. They had Gabe and Dad dead to rights with that alone. Do you think Mother would want you to continue the bloodshed?"

"Look Maria, you're getting into things you should stay away from. I'm serious. He's dangerous and nothing good is going to come from you meddling in this. Do you know where he is?"

"I'm not saying what I know or don't know, and I'm not going to help you find him," Maria said as she got up and stormed out of the room.

"Maria," Raph called after her, "we'll find him if the police don't find him first. You can be sure of that."

◆ ◆ ◆

"What's wrong?" Rose asked as Maria stormed out of the sunroom toward the kitchen.

"Sorry, just had a difficult conversation with my brother."

"I've had a few of those. Are you okay? Doesn't Raph like the funeral arrangements?"

"No, it wasn't about the funeral arrangements, it was about something else," Maria said.

"Listen, I don't know if it's related, but I heard someone say they know where Gabe is and something about a stakeout. Do you know anything about that?"

Maria squinted and sighed. "I think I need to go. Can you manage without me?" she asked, avoiding Rose's question.

Rose rubbed her chin. "That's fine, Maria. Sorry you can't stay, but thanks for coming. You did exactly what I wanted you to do."

Maria nodded, grabbed the lightweight cardigan she had brought, and walked out the front door. When she started her car, she turned on a local radio station that provided non-stop news. Within fifteen minutes, she heard what she was looking for. She pulled over to the side of the road and took out the burner phone Gabe had given her. She dialed his number.

"Gabe?" she said when he picked up.

"Hi Maria, is everything okay?" Gabe said.

"I just heard on the news that they are looking to question you in connection with a murder. Did you kill someone?"

"No. The victim was a friend of mine and he was loaning me an apartment. He was fixing my sink while I went out for a run. When I got back, he was dead. When I mentioned to you before that Raph had made an attempt on my life, this is what I was talking about. I didn't want to upset you with the details."

"How do you know it was Raph's people?" Maria asked.

"I'm sure it was them. I know they were in the area at the time of the killing."

"Then why are the police looking for you?"

"They must have found my fingerprints in the apartment and when they checked my background, I guess I was an obvious suspect. But I can prove Phil Morino and another guy were close by before and after the killing. Your brother's organization doesn't have any business in that area so they must have been sent there to find me. They would have killed me if I had been home."

Maria's throat tightened up and she began to breathe rapidly as she realized she had stood next to Phil Morino at Raph's house and he had tried to flirt with her. "So you're saying Phil Morino was the one who killed the man in the apartment?"

"I don't know which one pulled the trigger, but Phil was there."

Maria was so shocked she couldn't say anything.

"Are you okay?" Gabe asked.

"Yeah," she said. "Just give me a minute." She took a tissue out of her purse and wiped the tears from her eyes.

"Gabe, I just left a wake for my mother at Raph's. Rose said she heard some of his men saying they know where you are," she said tearfully. "You need to leave the condo."

"Okay, but if they know I'm here, they've got somebody watching. Where are you right now?"

"I'm almost back to Maple Grove. What are you going to do?"

"I'll think of something. I'll call you back in a few minutes."

CHAPTER 19

At about seven thirty the next morning, Maria pulled her small SUV into a parking space several blocks from her mother's condo. The local streets had come to life with traffic and people walking to their cars or train station to head into center city. Maria got out of her car dressed in baggy pants and a hoodie pulled down low to hide as much of her face as possible. A pair of large sunglasses covered most of her face that the hoodie didn't. She also carried a cane, the type older people would buy from a medical supply store. Gabe had told her the best time to leave was in the early morning, not only due to the increased traffic, but also because whoever was watching the building for signs of him would change shifts at around eight. As Maria turned the corner toward the entrance to the condo, she walked slowly with the cane. When she entered the condo building, she took her hood and sunglasses off and approached the front desk.

"Hi, I'm Maria D'Angelo. I've got to go up to my mother's condo."

"Hello Ms. D'Angelo. I heard about your mother and I'm sorry for your loss," the man behind the desk said. "If there's anything you need, let me know."

"Thank you. As a matter of fact, I'm picking up some stuff and I may need help lifting a box into my car."

"Of course, I'd be happy to help."

◆   ◆   ◆

About fifteen minutes later, Maria came down in the elevator with a large trunk on a dolly she could barely maneuver due to the weight of the trunk. Somehow, she managed to get it to the lobby and wheeled it to the front desk.

"If I bring my car around, could you help me load this in the back?" Maria asked.

"Sure thing, ma'am. Jose the doorman will help us as well."

"Okay, I'll be back in a few minutes," Maria said as she joined a group of about five people leaving the lobby. In about five minutes, she pulled a gray Toyota Land Cruiser up to the front door. Maria slowly got out of the vehicle with her hoodie and sunglasses in place and walked to the door with her cane to flag the doorman. A moment later, the front desk clerk and doorman lifted the trunk into the rear of the SUV. It barely fit, but they got it in and closed the liftgate door.

"That was heavy. Are you moving a set of barbells?" the doorman asked.

"Oh no, it's just books and files. They can be awfully heavy," Maria said. She handed each of them a twenty-dollar bill. "Thanks so much."

"Thank you very much. If you move furniture out, you'll need to reserve the service elevator. And remember, you can't move out on a Sunday," the desk clerk said.

Maria hopped into the driver's seat and began to drive. She wanted to leave the area as quickly as possible. She hoped the two men who had helped her didn't notice that she had covered part of the license plate with black duct tape, enough so no one could read the whole number.

"Everything okay back there?" Maria shouted to make sure Gabe could hear her. She heard three quick knocks on the inside of the trunk, their prearranged signal that there were no problems. She knew it was a tight fit and that Gabe must be very uncomfortable. "I'll drive a few minutes to make sure no one is following and then I'll pull over." Three more knocks.

Maria approached a small strip of stores that included a laundry, a Chinese restaurant, and a real estate office. She pulled around to the side lot out of view, lifted the rear hatch, and unlocked the trunk with a key. It flew open.

"Wow, thanks for the fresh air!" Gabe said. Maria strained as hard as she could to slide the trunk out of the opening so he could get up on his knees and climb out. Once he did, Maria brought the door down and Gabe hopped in the passenger side. Maria got in and they were off.

"Where did you say we were going?" he asked.

"My friend Julie is a real estate agent. She's got an empty house in Germantown. It belongs to an estate, so the owners won't be coming around. It should work until you figure out what you're going to do. No one in my family knows about the place, and I borrowed her car to get you there," Maria explained. "Not many buyers have asked to see the house, but if Julie needs to show it, she'll let us know."

"So you called her in the middle of the night?" Gabe asked.

"Yes. Three years ago, Julie was asked to leave the convent. She had no job and nowhere to go. My dad got my uncle to give her a job in one of his restaurants. We also got her a small apartment to stay in. While she was working at the restaurant, she studied for her real estate license and she's doing very well. She's so grateful, she'd do anything for me," Maria said.

"You're a good friend to have, Maria D'Angelo," Gabe said.

When they arrived, Maria handed Gabe a shopping bag with some soap, razors, and protein bars. She also had a large trash bag with some sheets, pillows, and a blanket. "This will tide you over. Julie said there's instant coffee in the cupboard. I'll bring more stuff when I have a chance, but I have to leave soon to meet with the funeral director," Maria said. "There is internet service in the house and the password is written on a card on the kitchen counter."

"You think of everything, Maria. I don't know how I can ever repay you for your help."

Maria walked Gabe to the front of the house and unlocked the door. It was an old house, furnished with just the basics and a bit run down, but it would do for Gabe's purposes. For a moment, Maria imagined living there and working with Gabe to fix the place up. It could be quite nice with a paint job and some new kitchen cabinets and appliances. Then she chided herself for such thoughts. She was with Brian now and was planning to see him this afternoon after meeting with the funeral director.

"When is the funeral?" Gabe asked.

"Saturday morning there's a mass at my mother's church in Chestnut Hill, then a graveside service at one."

"I wish I could come, but I don't think it would be a good idea right now."

"I understand," she said. "I don't know if you plan on going out, but there's a train station about a ten-minute walk from here. And Julie said she'd be glad to come by if you need help with anything in the house."

"It's probably best that she not come around, especially if I'm not here. This seems like a safe place, but you never know. Just be careful, Maria. Let me know if you think someone is following you. I think that's how they found me before—they were watching you."

A chill went up Maria's spine at the thought of her brother watching her. Raph would never hurt her … or would he? He had a score to settle and he was not one to let anything or anyone get in the way.

"Gabe," Maria said as she left, "remember that this arrangement is only for a few days and it would be best if you got out of town for a while."

"I'm working on it," he said.

CHAPTER 20

Dom sat in the car parked up the street from Carmella's condo building, and Frankie was positioned in the back alley where he could observe the loading dock and back doors. Frankie picked up his cell phone and dialed.

"Yeah," Dom answered.

"Anything going on out front? It's almost time to wrap up. Our replacements should be here by eight," Frankie said.

"Just lots of people coming and going. No sign of Gabe. The only thing unusual was an older woman drove up and the doorman helped load a big trunk into her car."

"How do you know she was older?"

"Well, she walked with a cane and kind of limped," Dom replied.

"And they helped her put a big thing in the back of an SUV? We better call the boss and report this," Frankie said.

"Nah, I'm sure it was nothing."

"If Gabe got away and you don't report it, you're gonna be in big trouble."

"Fine, I'll call."

Dom's hand shook as he tried to dial Raph's number. He finally got the number right on the third try. Raph picked up right away.

"Yeah, what's going on, Dom?"

"We're almost done here. It's been quiet. Only thing that happened this morning was an older woman drove up and the doorman and the guy in the lobby helped put a trunk in her SUV."

"Oh yeah? What did the woman look like?"

"I didn't get a good look. She was wearing sunglasses and a hoodie and she kind of kept her head low. There were a lot of people coming and going too."

"Did you follow her or at least get the license plate?"

"No. It didn't look like anything to me," Dom said.

"What kind of car was it?"

"It was a gray Toyota SUV. One of the larger ones."

"Don't leave. We're on our way over."

Raph threw the phone against the wall and it smashed into pieces. "Shit! This sounds just like something Gabe would do to sneak out of there," he said to Gus, who was sitting close by with a cup of coffee. "They loaded a trunk into a car driven by a woman who kept her face covered."

"So who do you think the woman was?"

"My sister, of course."

"She's still hot for Gabe?"

"Hot enough to take some big risks to help him. She doesn't realize what she's getting into."

"Does she realize that along with us, the police and FBI are looking for him? She could be charged as an accessory if she's hiding him," Gus said.

"Yeah. And Gabe might not react peacefully when one of us finds him. I've told her he's dangerous, but she won't listen to me."

A half hour later, Raph, Gus, Frankie, and Dom walked into the condo lobby. When Raph saw the clerk was the one he knew, he went up to the front desk.

"Mr. D'Angelo, to what do we owe the honor of a visit?" the clerk said.

"Hello Johnny. I need to go up and check on my mother's condo. These are some associates of mine."

"No problem."

"By the way, was my sister in this morning?"

"As a matter of fact, she was in before my shift began. She signed in here," Johnny said, pointing to the sign-in book. "Is there anything I can do to help?"

"No. We'll just go on up. Thanks."

The group rode the elevator to the second floor.

"I don't think he's here, but we don't know for sure. I'll open the door. Frankie and Dom, you guys go in and clear the place before we come in," Raph said with a smirk. He was not going to risk an encounter with Gabe if he was still in the unit.

Frankie and Dom entered cautiously with guns drawn. The moved into the foyer and around the corner.

"Bedrooms are clear," Dom said. A moment later, the two came back to the front. "It's all clear, boss," Dom said.

Raph and Gus entered.

"We were so close," Raph said, shaking his head.

"Do we know for sure that he was here?" Gus asked.

Raph picked up an envelope from the dining room table, addressed to "R. D'Angelo." He opened the envelope and found a greeting card with an ornamental cross on the front framed with a flowery design around the edges. There was nothing printed on the inside, just a handwritten message: "So sorry for your loss. Sincerely, G. Rossi."

"Yeah, he was here for sure."

CHAPTER 21

Maria parked her car and entered the Starbucks in Maple Grove. Brian was already there, standing at the front of line placing their orders.

"I ordered for you. The usual," Brian said.

"Don't you have to be at school now?" she asked as they sat down with their caffeine-laced drinks.

"I have a free first period so I can be a little late today. What about you?"

"I'm on bereavement leave this week. Technically I only get three days, but I added some personal days so I'm off all week."

Brian looked at Maria with a pained expression. "I'm sorry for what I did. I overreacted. Can you forgive me?"

"Yes, now that I understand why you felt the way you did," she said placing her hand on his arm. "You had some strong feelings when you saw Gabe and me together, and I was hurt when I couldn't reach you when my mother was dying. I hope we can both put this behind us," she said.

"How do we do that? Do we act like it never happened?"

"I'm not sure. Maybe there's some way we can get help."

"I'm certainly willing to do whatever it takes. I still love you," Brian said, looking up and wrinkling his forehead. "Is Gabe still in the picture?"

"Yes, but not the way you might think," Maria said, taking a sip of her drink. "Gabe is in trouble because my brother is trying to kill him."

"What?"

"Gabe broke the code of silence and Raph says he doesn't have any choice."

"There's always a choice," Brian said.

"I know that. But Raph is determined to kill Gabe, and I'm determined to prevent it."

"How are you going to do that? Raph works with some dangerous people, and it's not safe for you to get involved."

"I have a friend who is a realtor. She's letting Gabe stay in one of her listings. Before that, I let him stay in my mother's condo for a couple days. I moved Gabe when Raph somehow found out he was there," Maria said.

"I don't like this at all. You know that the police are looking for Gabe, don't you?"

"Yes, but he's innocent. He didn't kill or hurt anybody. I haven't given up on convincing Raph to back down. If I can convince Gabe to move away, I think Raph would let him go. But Gabe's a little stubborn."

"If the police consider him a suspect, you could get in trouble for hiding him."

"Gabe saved my life. I think I owe him a little help. Maybe you could help me help him."

"I don't know, Maria. I thought we came here to talk about our relationship."

"We *are* talking about it. I do care for you, Brian. I just need to be assured that you'll be there for me when I need you. That will do a lot for our relationship."

"Of course I'll be there. I saw something and I jumped to con-clusions. I won't do that again. As far as helping you protect Gabe, I don't know what I can do. I think you should be very careful. I like your idea of convincing him to leave town. It sounds like a win-win situation."

"Speaking of being there for me, will you come with me to the funeral on Saturday?"

"Of course."

CHAPTER 22

The crowd was larger than expected for Carmella D'Angelo's funeral mass. She had many friends from her church and the charitable organizations she and her husband had supported. Raph had invited a large number of his employees and friends, and word had spread throughout the D'Angelo organization that everyone needed to be present for the funeral service.

Maria sat in the first row near the center aisle, next to Brian, with relatives and friends surrounding her. Raph and his family sat in the front row on the opposite side of the aisle. Maria had arrived first, and when Raph came in, they didn't acknowledge one another, although Rose nodded at Maria when she entered the row.

Father Pierce gave a glowing sermon eulogizing Carmella's character, her faithfulness, and her good works in the community. There was no mention of her organized crime connections. After mass, the crowd shuffled downstairs to a fellowship hall where a buffet lunch was laid out. Raph and his family formed a receiving line at the entrance to the hall to greet those who attended. Maria and Brian were standing near one of the tables, and Rose left the line and approached them.

"Maria, come join the receiving line. You can stand next to me if you like."

Maria grabbed Brian by the arm and walked over to the line, where she stood with Rose and Brian between her and Raph. Maria knew a number of the priests and a few of the nuns who attended. She was sincerely grateful for their attendance and shook their hands with enthusiasm, even hugging a few of them. Maria hardly knew any of Raph's associates, but felt like she wanted to wash her hands after shaking theirs. At one point, Maria glanced over at Raph and they made eye contact. His stare was as cold as steel and made a chill run up her spine. Maria had always had a cordial relationship with her brother. *How did it sink to this level?* she wondered.

◆　◆　◆

At one o'clock the procession of cars reached the cemetery. The funeral home had provided separate limos for Raph's family and for Maria and Brian. The crowd was smaller, but there were probably still seventy or eighty people assembled graveside. In the rear of the crowd stood Special Agents Natalie Perez and Dennis McIntyre.

"Looks like the usual suspects," Agent Perez whispered. Both of them scanned the crowd as discreetly as they could to mark members of the D'Angelo crime family.

"So far, I don't see any sign of Rossi," Agent McIntyre said.

Perez and McIntyre had a third agent positioned at the tree line about a hundred feet away, scanning the crowd and the surrounding area with binoculars to see if Gabe had decided to show up.

"I'm not surprised," Perez said. "It would be like walking into a hornet's nest with this group."

"I've been watching Maria and Raphael D'Angelo since they arrived. They don't seem to be particularly friendly with one another," McIntyre said.

"I noticed the same thing. Makes you wonder what's going on in that family. We have to assume they both know Rossi is in the area.

Maria and Gabe had a real thing going before he was arrested. I can't imagine that she has the same attitude toward Gabe as the boss does."

"No doubt," Agent McIntyre agreed.

<h1 style="text-align:center">CHAPTER 23</h1>

It didn't take long for Gabe to become bored staying hidden in the house in Germantown. He'd watched the news on his laptop and heard repeated reports about the investigation of the murder in Warminster. He'd used up most of the provisions Maria had left for him in the kitchen and was ready for some variety. It was time for a change of scenery. Gabe's first thought was to survey the neighborhood so that he would have a good feel for the routes in and out. He donned his gym clothes and a baseball cap and headed out for a run before sunrise.

First, Gabe carefully scanned the area around his borrowed home to make sure no one was watching. He knew the D'Angelo family didn't have any dealings in the Germantown area that they could use as a base for observation. Of course, all it would take would be one of their soldiers in a parked car with a pair of binoculars. After taking in the surroundings, he slowly jogged a few blocks over to Germantown Avenue, the street that would take him to Chestnut Hill if he travelled north on it a few miles. Gabe took note of the small commercial establishments on the avenue—a pizza parlor, a bike shop, and several small grocery stores. He would return to the grocery stores when they opened, and maybe the pizza parlor in the evening. After heading north for seven or eight blocks, Gabe turned west on one of the cross streets and ran until he hit Lincoln Drive, a steep, curvy road that wound through a ravine in Wissahickon Valley Park. Gabe crossed the street and entered the park at one of the trailheads. He had spent time in the park growing up and had gone jogging there many times when he was in college. There was a complex series of trails, and if you didn't know your way around, it would be easy to get lost. If anyone from the D'Angelo family tried to track him down while he was there, he could ditch them in the trails.

Gabe made his way down to a trail that ran along the east side of Wissahickon Creek and ran north until he came to a spot known as "Devil's Pool." There was a small tributary that flowed into Wissahickon Creek with a deep, rocky pool less than a hundred feet off the main trail. It was a popular swimming hole for young people to use in the summer to cool off, but this time of year, the place was deserted. Gabe himself had come to the spot many times when he was a teenager, and it brought back many memories. He preferred to come during times like this, before the summer crowds arrived. The peacefulness and beauty of the spot always provided a place of solace for Gabe from the pressures of life. Gabe had even gone there with Raph to plunge into the cool waters after running in the park on a hot day.

Gabe walked up the rocky creek bed and began to climb up the steep boulder-strewn hill that framed both sides of the pool. When he got high enough, he noticed he had enough of a signal on his burner phone to make or receive a call. Gabe had been thinking about making a certain call for several days and decided it was time to go for it. He sat on a log and dialed a number. Gabe waited nervously for someone to pick up. Finally, he heard a voice.

"This is the field office of the Federal Bureau of Investigation in Kansas City, Missouri," the recorded voice said. Gabe listened to the menu choices and hit the button for the parole office.

"Federal parole office."

"I'd like to speak to Carl Kramer, please," Gabe said.

"Let me connect you."

A moment later, Parole Officer Kramer picked up. "This is Kramer."

"It's Randy Sherman," Gabe said, using the name given to him in the witness protection program.

"Ah, Mr. Sherman, I've been waiting to hear from you. I see you're not using the cell phone you received when you entered the program."

"Sorry, I must have misplaced it," Gabe needed to proceed cautiously. He assumed Kramer knew about his absence, but he wasn't sure what else. He quickly found out.

"You should know that the FBI is looking for you, and I understand the police in Pennsylvania are also looking for you," Kramer said, then paused to let Gabe answer.

"Well, most of it is based on a misunderstanding."

"My advice to you would be to turn yourself in. It's pretty clear you've left the jurisdiction you were assigned, and that's a violation of your parole conditions. Are you willing to do that? The longer you're gone, the worse it'll be for you."

"I need you to know that I didn't kill anybody. I've seen the news and the police are wrong. Andy Carr was a good friend of mine. The person responsible for his death was Raphael D'Angelo, head of the mafia in Philadelphia."

"You can tell your whole story when you come back into the system."

"I can't. Raphael has a contract out on my life. I was borrowing an apartment from Andy and Raph's men came when I was out running. I can prove that they were there."

"Again, you need to come back in and tell your story."

"Have the FBI check the surveillance cameras at the Starbucks on York Road in Warminster, Pennsylvania. You'll see the D'Angelo hit team there shortly before and soon after they killed Carr. I've got some other physical evidence as well." Gabe looked at this watch. He didn't want the call to go more than two minutes in case they were set up to trace his location. "The D'Angelo family has a lot of pull. If I'm in custody, they can still get to me."

"I'm sure the FBI can keep you safe," Kramer said.

Gabe knew he wouldn't win an argument with a parole officer, so he decided to wrap up the call. He had told Kramer what he wanted him to know. "Thanks for hearing me out. I need to go now. I'll try to contact you again."

After disconnecting the call, Gabe quickly removed the battery from the phone. Then he pulled out the sim card, crushed it on the rock with his shoe, and threw it and the phone into the middle of the Devil's Pool.

CHAPTER 24

"You notice anything about the boss? Seems to me he hasn't been himself," Phil Morino said as he walked away from the graveside service.

"He just lost his mother," Gus Nasuti answered as he fiddled in his pocket for his car keys.

"No, this isn't about his mother. I've known Raph for a long time and he was never that close to his mother. I think it's about his sister. When he found out she smuggled Gabe into his mother's condo, and then smuggled him out, it's like he got a little crazy. He and I used to talk all the time. Now, he hasn't said a word to me since before the wake," Phil said. "And he drank a lot more than usual at the wake."

"Maybe he's upset with you for letting Gabe get away."

"I didn't let Gabe get away. I mean, we had to get rid of the guy at the apartment. But didn't that make Gabe look guilty?"

"It's water under the bridge. Question is, what do we do now?" Gus asked.

"I think Raph's sister knows where Gabe is. Maybe there's a way we can get her to talk," Phil said.

"Do you really want to go there? I mean she's the boss's sister."

"Does he even need to know?" asked Phil, standing by Gus's car.

"I don't like the idea of putting the squeeze on a family member, especially the family member of the boss. You should really get his okay on this before proceeding." Gus got in his car and rolled down the window.

"Okay, just forget it," Phil said, already figuring out a way to do this without involving the boss.

As Gus drove off, Phil saw Denny Delvato walking toward the area where several cars were parked.

"Denny!" Phil shouted, gesturing for Denny to come his way.

"What's up?" Denny asked.

"I need your help on something that I think will make the boss very happy if we can pull it off. Do you know Maria, the boss's sister?"

"Only what I've heard about her. She was at the boss's house the other night for the wake. She's really hot."

"I figured you'd zero right in on that. We think she knows where Rossi is."

"So you want me to get her and bring her to the warehouse?" Denny asked.

The warehouse was an abandoned building near the clubhouse in South Philadelphia that the D'Angelo family sometimes used. It wasn't on anybody's radar. More than a few times, they had taken recalcitrant soldiers there to teach them a lesson. They had even killed a few people there.

"No, nothin' like that. I was thinking more in terms of a friendly social call. But first, I need you to find out some stuff for me. What I need is Maria's home address and where she works. Also, it looks like she's got a boyfriend, the guy who came to the funeral with her. Find out who he is, where he lives, where he works, et cetera." Phil knew Denny was not only good with weapons but also highly skilled at using the computer for investigative purposes.

"Sure thing. How soon do you need this?" Denny asked.

"Put a rush on it. We want to find Gabe as soon as possible. As I said, if we can do this, the boss will be very happy. And let's just keep this between you and me for now."

Chapter 25

Special Agent Natalie Perez called a meeting of the organized crime task force at the Philadelphia field office. Once the whole team was there, she took a sip of coffee, opened her file, and looked at the agents sitting around the table before she spoke. "A few weeks ago, we discussed Gabriel Rossi and his apparent absence from the witness protection program in Missouri. We thought he might return to the area, and apparently that's what happened. We did an extensive search of CCTV footage in and around the neighborhood where he used to live and we got one possible hit of him leaving a bar on Lombard Street. Now, as you know, we've also placed him at a crime scene in Warminster, about thirty miles north of here. The local police are looking for Mr. Rossi but their resources are limited. We've stepped in to help but haven't come up with much in the way of leads on where to find him. However, Rossi's parole officer in Kansas City received a phone call yesterday from him."

"Do we know where Rossi was when he made the call?" Agent Reed asked.

"Our surveillance people believe the call came from Wissahickon Valley Park near the Germantown section of Philadelphia. It was a short call, so we don't have anything more specific than that."

"That's a pretty large park. I think we have to assume Rossi made the call from the park to make it harder for us to get his location. I'm gonna guess that the signals from the phone went dead after the call," Agent McIntyre said.

"That's correct. I'm sure Rossi destroyed the phone after the call, which confirms our profile that he is savvy and knows what he's doing. There are only a few spots in the park with good phone reception, so we sent a team out to have a look around, but they haven't found anything. As of this time, Rossi could be anywhere in the city, or maybe even out of the city. We've gotten the Philadelphia PD involved and they've put out an all-points bulletin on him." Agent Perez picked up some papers from her folder. "The main reason for this meeting is that Rossi told his parole officer he didn't commit the murder in Warminster. He claims he was a friend of the victim and that he was borrowing the apartment. He said he was the intended victim, but that the D'Angelo family killed the victim instead."

"Does he have any corroborating evidence of that?" Agent Reed asked.

"As a matter of fact, he does. Rossi told the parole officer to check the surveillance camera at the Starbucks about five minutes from the crime scene. We got the local police to pull the video, and it shows two prominent members of the D'Angelo family were there. We've got surveillance images of Phil Morino, who is reputed to be Raphael D'Angelo's number two boss, and a Dennis Delvato, who is considered a top soldier and the family's inside hit man. That plus a transparent motive—retribution for Rossi's testimony against the D'Angelo family at the trial three years ago—and we have a plausible alternative theory for investigating the murder."

"And a basis of reasonable doubt for Rossi's defense lawyer to argue if the state authorities charge him with murder," Reed added.

"Does this mean Rossi is no longer a suspect in the murder?" one of the younger agents asked.

"Even though Rossi has suggested a plausible scenario, we're not just taking his word for it, and neither are the local police. Rossi is a convicted felon with a history of violence and he can be placed at the murder scene. Because of this, and because Rossi has violated his parole conditions, we have obtained a warrant for his arrest and are working with local police and the Pennsylvania State Police," Agent Perez said.

"So what are we doing to find this guy" Agent Reed asked.

"As I mentioned, local and state law enforcement are actively looking for him alongside of us. Incidentally, I should report that Agent McIntyre and I attended a funeral service on Saturday for Carmella D'Angelo. She was the wife of Michael D'Angelo and the mother of Raphael D'Angelo. Not surprisingly, there was no sign of Rossi at the funeral, but we did lay eyes on Phil Morino. I assume Delvato was also there, but we didn't have the surveillance footage then and had no reason to look for him," Agent Perez said as she straightened some papers in her file. "That's about all I have. So let's double down and find Rossi. If we don't find him before the D'Angelo family does, there will be another murder to investigate."

CHAPTER 26

Gabe sat in the kitchen of his borrowed home eating a frozen pizza he had heated up in the oven. He flicked on the TV to see if there was any news, but there was nothing about him or the investigation of the murder in Warminster. They had moved on to other stories, which was fine with Gabe. He knew the FBI and police would still be looking for him even though he had directed them toward some plausible evidence that he wasn't the murderer. He was still a former mafia informant who had violated his parole, and that was enough to motivate the Feds. And of course, the D'Angelo soldiers would all be combing the streets and looking for clues to his whereabouts.

Despite the danger, Gabe was tired of being cooped up in the house. He jumped in the shower and got dressed, donning a hoodie and a baseball cap to help hide his features. About ten minutes later, he entered a small tavern on Germantown Avenue. It was nothing fancy, but it was a dimly lit, cozy little joint, and he felt it was as safe as anywhere. Gabe knew it wasn't a hangout for the D'Angelos or any of their friends. Gabe sat at the bar. A large mirror on the wall behind the bar gave him a pretty good view of the whole establishment, and there were only a few patrons present.

"How about those Phillies?" the bartender asked as he poured Gabe a Yuengling on draft.

"Huh?" Gabe said as if he had been deep in thought.

"Did you see last night's game? Nola shut out the Mets," the bartender said.

"No. Sorry. I must have been busy." Gabe thought about the sports bets the Phillies players had placed with him through a trainer who acted as a middleman. Back then, Gabe could get as many free tickets as he wanted to the games.

"They're only a game out of first place behind Atlanta, and the Braves are coming into town next week. Should be a good series," the bartender continued. "It's still early in the season. Never know what could happen."

Gabe remained silent. He didn't really feel like talking about baseball right now, and the bartender seemed to get the message as he took a rag and began wiping down the other end of the bar. Gabe's mind began to wander as he slowly sipped his beer. He couldn't help remembering that three years ago he was flying high. He had become a close confidante of Michael D'Angelo and was on track to become a made man in the organization. It was actually Michael's idea to have Gabe distract Maria from her activities at the convent and give her second thoughts about becoming a nun, but he hadn't planned on Gabe and Maria falling in love. Now Gabe had Maria close by again, and she was helping him, but he didn't have her heart. He'd need to win it all over again.

Gabe looked up when the bartender tapped him on the shoulder. "Another Yuengling?" the bartender asked.

Gabe hadn't realized his mug was empty. "Sure."

As the bartender refilled his glass, Gabe realized a woman had slipped onto the barstool next to him. She appeared to be a few years older, but she was a knockout, with a low-cut dress and dark, luxurious, shoulder-length tresses.

"What's wrong, you get stood up by your date?" she asked, leaning in so close he could smell her perfume.

"Uh no," Gabe said. "Just taking a break after a busy week." He took a long swig of his beer.

"We could all use a break once in a while," she replied.

Despite his feelings for Maria, Gabe couldn't help feeling attracted to the woman. He thought she could be a prospect if things didn't work out with Maria, then reminded himself that he had told Maria he was a changed man, not the kind of guy who played fast and loose with women. Still, he reasoned as he gave her another look, it wouldn't hurt to have a woman like this as a friend.

"My name is Gabe, by the way," he said, immediately regretting the use of his real name. Gabe reminded himself he couldn't let his guard down even in a seemingly safe place.

"I'm Lucy," she answered, putting out her soft, silky hand to shake Gabe's. "I kind of got stood up. Maybe we were meant to meet up."

"Do you live around here?" Gabe could hardly believe he was being so forward.

"Not far," she said. "I'm a trainer at a gym a couple of blocks down the avenue. So, what's your business?"

"I've been involved in management of casinos and resorts."

"Is that what's kept you busy this week?"

"Not really. I've been out of town and I've got some family matters to clear up."

"Well, I'm glad you're back," she said softly, placing her hand on Gabe's. "Shall we finish our drinks and get out of here?"

The beer was starting to have its effect, and Gabe felt a strong urge to leave with this woman, even just to blow off some steam. But he began to see red flags popping up. *Who is she? Could she be an informant for the FBI, or maybe an undercover police officer?* With her fit and trim body, Gabe could picture her in a uniform with her hair pulled back in a bun. It wasn't the first time Gabe had been hit on by an older woman, but something about this seemed a little strange.

"Say, it's been great meeting you, but I gotta be somewhere and have to go. Do you come here a lot?"

"You're leaving? You sure you need to go right away? I live only a few blocks from here," Lucy said.

"I'm afraid so." Gabe drained his mug. "Maybe some other time. I mean that," he said, getting up from the barstool and leaving two twenty-dollar bills. "This covers my drinks and hers," Gabe told the bartender as he started to walk away. He didn't know how many drinks Lucy had before they met, but he was pretty sure forty dollars would cover them plus a generous tip.

"Thanks, buddy."

When the bartender replied, Gabe realized being a large tipper was not the best way to keep a low profile. Ideally, the bartender would have forgotten Gabe even came in, but now he would remember for sure.

Before he could step away from the bar, Lucy spoke up. "Gabe, it was nice to meet you." She handed him a business card. The card listed her full name as "Lucy Smith Thomason" and identified her as a "Licensed Personal Fitness Trainer" at "Avenue Fitness." It had a business phone number printed on it and she had written her personal cell phone number.

"Thanks," Gabe said as he turned and walked out. On the way home, he passed Avenue Fitness. It took up twice the space of the other businesses that fronted Germantown Avenue. Maybe she really was who she said she was, and not an informant for the mafia or the government. Still, Gabe had to be diligent about keeping a low profile. You could never be too careful.

Chapter 27

Brian lived in a small house that he rented on Inman Terrace, just off York Road in Maple Grove. It was nothing fancy, but it was conveniently located less than ten minutes from the high school where he taught, and the rent was low enough to allow him to begin saving to buy a house. He knew most of the neighbors that were close by, and he even taught some of their kids in his classes. Because he used the garage to store the junk he had accumulated over that past several years, he parked his silver Hyundai Elantra in the small driveway in front of the garage. Today, however, when he pulled in around four o'clock, he noticed a large black SUV parked across the street about three car lengths up from his driveway. It appeared to be a luxury model, like a Cadillac Escalade, but he couldn't tell for sure.

What was clear was that this vehicle was not from the neighborhood. It just didn't fit in. The windows were darkened so Brian couldn't see who, if anyone, was inside. He didn't give much thought to it as he grabbed his canvas briefcase and walked toward the front door. On the way, Brian stooped to grab a branch that had fallen on the walkway. Then he opened the mailbox on the wall next to the front door. He paused for a moment to skim through the letters and glossy junk mail folders that would be quickly consigned to the trash.

Before going inside, Brian glanced toward the street for no particular reason. When he did, he saw a window on the passenger side of the SUV closing. He hadn't seen it open, but it was definitely closing. *Maybe they wanted to throw a cigarette butt out,* he thought. *Or maybe they photographed me.* Brian was not a suspicious person, but knowing Maria's connection to some unsavory characters made him a little wary. Could this be some of the people he saw at the party for Maria's niece? If so, why would they be watching him? Was it to see what kind of person might someday become related to the D'Angelo family by marriage? Maybe they didn't like him and wanted to keep him away from Maria. Were they planning to "whack" him, as they say? That seemed a little ridiculous. Brian hadn't even proposed to her yet, and given the events of the last week, that whole process might be delayed while he and Maria worked out some issues between them. Brian had read some articles about the mafia and recalled they rarely took action against family members, at least those not involved in the business.

Maybe he was letting his imagination run a little too wild. Either way, it was time to go into the house and start on some of the work he brought with him from school. As the assistant football coach, Brian was responsible for placing orders for equipment the team would need in the coming season. Football was months away, but equipment with team colors and symbols had long lead times, and Brian couldn't afford to wait any longer.

After an hour at the desk in the spare bedroom upstairs, Brian decided to stretch his legs. He got up and walked over to the window looking out on the street. The black SUV was in the back of his mind, and he wanted to see if it was still there. What he saw shocked him a bit. Not only was the SUV still there, but it had pulled up right in front of his driveway. The window rolled down—the same window he thought he had seen closing. It was hard to see inside the car, but Brian was sure he saw the dark silhouette of someone with a camera.

Given the location of the SUV and its open window, the only thing they could be photographing was his car.

Why would anyone want photos of my car and license plate? A chill went up Brian's spine. He ran downstairs, grabbed his iPhone from the kitchen counter, and headed toward the front door. His plan was to get a picture of the black SUV and its license plate, but when he went outside it was gone. Brian stepped back in and locked the deadbolt. Then he went to the kitchen and made sure the back door was locked.

He called Maria. "Hey," he said when she picked up. "Something really weird just happened."

"There's a lot of weird stuff going on right now. What happened?"

"A big, black SUV was parked on my street when I got home. I looked over when I was getting the mail and saw a window closing. Then, about an hour later, I looked out my upstairs window and they were right in front of my driveway, and I saw someone take a picture of my car."

"That is strange," Maria said. "Are you up to date on your car payments?"

"Of course I am. Do you think it could be someone from your family?"

"Brian, anything is possible with my family right now. I wouldn't worry too much about it though. You have nothing to do with anything that's going on and they don't bother family members."

"I guess you're right. We'll talk again soon." Brian said.

CHAPTER 28

Special Agent Dennis McIntyre drove past the neatly kept townhomes on Vernon Street in South Philadelphia with Agent Perez riding shotgun. Dennis glanced at the GPS on his dashboard.

"We should be close," he said.

"Looks like it's right up here," Agent Perez said, pointing to a unit several doors up. "You can start looking for a parking spot. I'd rather not double park and make this a big production."

"Here we go. This spot is only about a block away." Dennis pulled into the parking spot and the agents got out.

"Doesn't look like a high crime area, does it?"

"You know what they say. The neighborhoods where mafia bosses live are the safest in the city. They don't tolerate street crime around here, and the criminal element knows that."

"This is it," Perez said as they walked up the steps and rang the bell.

In a moment, a middle-aged woman with greying hair pulled back opened the door. She was wearing an apron and looked as though the visit was interrupting something important in the kitchen.

"Hello, I'm Special Agent Natalie Perez with the FBI. This is my partner, Agent McIntyre. Is Mr. Morino in? I mean Mr. Phil Morino?"

The woman, Mrs. Morino, stood staring at them for a moment as if she was wondering what to say. Just then a voice boomed from inside the home. "It's okay, Angela, tell them I'll be right there."

"Good morning," Phil said as he came to the door. "Would you like to come in?"

"Yes, we won't take much of your time. We'd just like to see if you can help us with some information," Perez said.

"Angela, could you bring us some coffee and pastries?" Phil shouted toward the kitchen.

"Oh, no thanks, Mr. Morino. We're good."

"I can't imagine what I could help you with, but go ahead and ask."

"Are you familiar with a man named Gabriel Rossi?" Perez asked.

"I've heard of him but don't really know him," Morino said, raising his eyebrows and pursing his lips. Despite the fact that the agents declined refreshments, Angela brought in a tray of coffee and some fancy looking Italian pastry.

"Have you seen him recently?" Perez asked.

"Can't say that I have. I thought he was out of town."

"How would you know that?" Perez asked.

"He used to live around here. Ya know, this is South Philadelphia, but our neighborhood is like a small town where everybody knows everyone else, at least on some level."

Agent Perez decided to grab one of the cups of coffee, despite her earlier refusal.

"This is very good coffee," she said, trying to relax the atmosphere a little.

"Well, you're in Little Italy. We know how to make good coffee here. You should try Angela's expresso," Phil said.

"I assume you're aware that Mr. Rossi used to work for Michael D'Angelo?" she asked.

"I think I've heard that," Phil replied, keeping his answers skillfully short.

"And he testified against Mr. D'Angelo at his trial. You recall that, don't you?" she asked.

"I wasn't at the trial," Phil answered, pursing his lips again as he picked up his coffee cup.

"Are you acquainted with Raphael D'Angelo, the son of Michael D'Angelo?" Perez asked.

"What can I say? Everyone around here knows of the D'Angelos. Some of his relations live on this street."

"Since you seem to be plugged in to this neighborhood, there are rumors that Raphael D'Angelo has a contract on the life of Gabriel Rossi," Perez continued. "Can you confirm that rumor?"

"There are always rumors. I tend not to dwell on them." Phil rubbed his chin.

"I mean, you work pretty high up in the D'Angelo organization. If there was such a contract, you would know about it, wouldn't you?" Perez asked.

"Again, I don't want to speculate about such things," Morino stared coldly at the agents. "It's been a pleasure talking to you both, but I really must get back to work here. My grandchildren are coming and I need to help Angela get ready," Phil said as he stood up and gestured toward the door.

Perez was surprised Morino had talked as much as he had. The agents stood, and Morino began walking them to the front door. "Oh, one more thing. Were you and Dennis Delvato in Warminster last Tuesday morning?"

Morino grimaced. "As I said, I need to get back to work. Have a great day."

◆　◆　◆

"Did you see the look on his face when you asked if he knew Rossi?" McIntyre asked as the two walked toward their car.

"Yep. He had some reaction to all the questions after that. He was clearly uncomfortable. That's why he was so anxious to get rid of us."

"So what's your takeaway?"

"This isn't Morino's first rodeo," Perez said. "He's been questioned before. He was extremely careful not to admit or deny questions relating to the murder or his being present at the scene. He knows that lying to a federal officer is a felony. My gut feeling is that Rossi was correct. They were there to kill him and they killed the wrong guy, but we don't have enough evidence to arrest him."

CHAPTER 29

Maria was finishing up her day at school when her phone buzzed. "Hi Brian," she said when she saw his name on the caller ID.

"Hey Maria," he said in a cheerful voice. "Remember when we postponed our dinner date before Tessa's party?"

"Yes. I'm sorry I had to cancel."

"Well, a lot has happened since then. Can we do it tonight, I mean go to the same restaurant?"

"Sure. That sounds good."

"Look, I know you've been through a lot and we had some issues come up. Let's just hit the reset button and enjoy each other's company."

"That sounds good. I need a break."

◆　◆　◆

Brian picked Maria up at seven, and they arrived at the restaurant about fifteen minutes later. It was a weeknight, so they were seated right away.

Brian opened the menu and began to read it. "I'm still puzzled by the mysterious SUV I saw last night."

"Did you see anything else strange?" Maria asked.

"No. I saw it around seven last night and nothing since. Do you think your brother is trying to harass you through me? I mean, he knows you helped Gabe, right?"

"He knows I helped Gabe, but I can't believe he would drag you or me into something," Maria said.

"True, but maybe he thinks you've injected yourself into the situation." Brian closed the menu and looked at Maria. "Let's just split a small pizza and get side salads, okay?"

"That's fine. But going back to what you said, I haven't dragged myself into anything. Gabe is just trying to live his life. If I help him, that's not putting myself in the middle of my brother's unsavory business," Maria said with a frown on her face.

"Whoa. I'm not accusing you. I'm just trying to see this from Raph's perspective, as distorted as that may be."

"So what do I do?"

"What you said before. You need to convince Gabe to leave town. He'll never be safe here, and if he's not safe, you may be in danger as well. Or, maybe you should turn Gabe into the police. If he didn't commit the murder in Warminster, he should be okay, right?"

"I could never betray a friend. If he's in jail or prison, he's still in danger. You have no idea what my brother can do. He's got friends in prison who owe him. It would be putting Gabe in a situation more dangerous than what he's in right now," Maria said as the server brought their drinks.

"Well, what kind of trouble is he in if he didn't commit the murder? All he did was leave witness protection. I looked through some civics textbooks we use at the high school. If he's on parole and skips out, it's a violation of his parole or probation. He might go back to jail for a short time, but he'd be in federal prison. Maybe he could work out a deal. He agrees to turn himself in if he's placed in a safer prison far away from here, maybe one of those minimum-security prisons. That would sure be better than living his life on the run."

"I don't know, Brian. He's pretty stubborn. I don't know if I can convince him to leave."

"Well, you and your brother are also a little stubborn. What if Raph won't back down? Just remember, he can't look weak to the people who work for him. Sooner or later, either Raph or the Feds are going to catch Gabe. Then he won't have much leverage to negotiate a deal. And maybe he'll still be facing murder charges for the killing in Warminster. Just because he told you he's innocent doesn't mean the police around here will believe him."

Maria picked up a napkin and began wiping her lips.

"You've hardly touched your food," Brian said as he started on his third piece of pizza.

"I guess I'm not that hungry," A tear started to roll down Maria's cheek, and she put her face in her hands. "I hate living like this, knowing that someone who saved me once is in danger. I know he made some bad choices in the past but I honestly believe he wants to walk away from that."

"You're a good person, and that's the reason I love you. But you also need to think about your own safety. I really worry about you sometimes."

"Okay. I'll talk to Gabe and tell him he really needs to leave town. But where can he go?"

"I guess that's up to him. If I had people like Raph chasing me, I'd find somewhere—anywhere—where I could cool my heels for a while."

"Okay. I'll keep encouraging him to leave. I don't want anything to happen to him, but I really want to get back to a normal life," Maria said, wondering if Brian's goal was just to get Gabe out of town and far from her.

♦ ♦ ♦

Brian dropped Maria at her townhome near the train station in Maple Grove. It was a great location, less than five minutes by car from her school and minutes away from grocery shopping and a large shopping mall named after the old amusement park that was there before. It was also close to Brian's rental house. When she got inside, she retrieved the burner phone Gabe had given her.

"Hi Maria, what's up?" he said when he picked up.

"Just checking in. And I wanted to ask you about your plans. I think you know that Julie's listing is not a permanent solution."

"I know. I'm still working on my plans."

"Maybe it's time to think about getting out of town. You can't go on living here on the run. It's also a lot of pressure on me, knowing that my brother is looking for you. What I'm saying is, you need to get serious about leaving. Maybe you can come back someday, but now's not a good time."

"I hear you."

"If you hear me, what can I tell Julie? She says she's getting some calls asking about the house and she's going to need to show it soon."

"If I get an hour's warning, I can be cleared out of here during her showings."

"Julie's doing me a favor by letting you stay there. She's taking a big risk. If the owners ever found out, they'd fire her, and she could even lose her license."

"Can she give me a few days?" Gabe asked. "I've got some things I need to do that might help the situation. And no, I'm not going to hurt anyone." Gabe said.

"Okay. Gabe, I want you to know that I care about you and don't want anything to happen to you. Right now I just don't have a lot of influence over my brother. I wish I did, but I don't." Maria paused. "Please get away from here as soon as you can. It's for your own good."

"Maria, thank you so much for all you've done. I know you care. I'm sorry I'm causing problems, and I'll do my best to stop doing that."

"Thanks, Gabe. How are you doing otherwise? Is there anything you need?" she asked.

"I'm okay for now. There are several small shops nearby that I can sneak out and go to. I'm not setting any routines that anyone could notice. I'll be okay," he said. "How about if I call you in a day or so?"

"That's fine," Maria said.

CHAPTER 30

Gabe decided to get moving on his next steps. He wasn't optimistic his plan would work, but it was worth trying. He had checked the train schedules and found that the commuter trains started running at five thirty, when it was barely light. Gabe left the house a few minutes after five the next morning. He was confident none of the D'Angelo soldiers would be out of bed, much less looking for him. It was only a ten-minute walk to the train station and he waited about ten more minutes before the first train arrived. Gabe was surprised at how many people were up and on such an early train to the city. It was fine since he wanted to blend into the crowd. He wore sunglasses along with his new mustache and beard stubble he had grown the last several days to alter his normally clean-cut appearance.

Gabe found himself on a nearly full rail car headed to Jefferson Station on Market Street in center city. Despite the crowded car, the half hour ride was pleasant and brought back memories as it passed through the stops near Temple University where he had attended. When he arrived, he took the elevator to the street level and found a small café along Market Street. He sat drinking a coffee and eating a muffin to kill some time. This would be his most dangerous foray since leaving the witness protection program, as he was headed deep into the heart of the city where the D'Angelo family members walked the streets for their various enterprises—some legal, but most not. He sat in the rear of the coffee shop and held a newspaper that covered most of his face and allowed him to glance over the top to keep an eye on who was coming in or out.

In addition to the risk of running into the D'Angelo family, Gabe was only about six blocks west of the federal courthouse, which held the United States' Attorneys offices. A block north of the courthouse, on Arch Street, was the building where the FBI offices were located. He doubted anyone from those places would recognize him today, but he needed to be careful. Gabe decided he would stay as long as he could in the coffee shop, then when the streets filled up with commuters, he'd have cover to move a few blocks south. He had to arrive at his destination a few minutes before ten, so he had some hours to kill.

♦ ♦ ♦

At seven thirty, when the streets were full of pedestrians walking to their jobs, Gabe made his move, walking two blocks south to Walnut Street near Washington Square. Gabe looked up and down the street until he found another coffee shop he could sit in for a while. When he found one, there were a number of nurses and medical personnel who were stopping in at the end of their shift for the energy needed to travel home before crashing for the day. As he drank another cup, he decided if he needed to come back to this part of the city, which was near Jefferson Hospital, medical scrubs would make a good disguise, but it was too late for that today.

After finishing his coffee, Gabe decided to check the street. There were still a lot of pedestrians, and he felt he couldn't stay longer in the coffee shop because he would become noticeable to the people working behind the counter—something he wanted to avoid. He left a tip on the table and walked outside and down the street to Washington Square, a small city park, where he found an empty bench. Gabe lifted his newspaper and resumed waiting. His plan had been to travel on the train early and blend in with the weekly commuters. Now he wondered if he could have taken a later train and disappeared just as easily. Either way, he was now entering the final phases of his plan. *It's now or never,* he thought. Gabe pulled out a smart phone, hit the Uber app icon, and punched in a request for a ride to Ninth and Christian Streets in South Philadelphia. It was time to enter enemy territory. In about six minutes, a small Nissan SUV pulled up to the square and Gabe, using the name Bruno Conti, slid into the back seat.

"Another beautiful day in the city!" the driver said as Gabe closed the door.

"It sure is," said Gabe.

CHAPTER 31

At exactly ten o'clock, Raphael D'Angelo entered Tony's Barber Shop on Christian Street to get his weekly trim, along with a shave. Gabe was already standing in a dimly lit hallway in the shop that led to a bathroom and supply closet in the rear. When Raph entered, he was alone in the front of the shop. This wasn't unusual since Tony, the aging proprietor, frequently went out for a coffee or to smoke. A few minutes before Raph arrived, Gabe had told Tony he was in town to surprise his old friend, Raph, and given him a hundred-dollar bill to walk a block and a half to an Italian bakery to pick up an order of cannoli. Tony was happy to oblige since Gabe had told him he could keep the change.

Raph hung his sport coat on a coat hanger across from the barber chairs. Gabe knew from past experience that Raph likely had a small pistol in the pocket of the coat he had just hung up, but as far as he could tell, Raph wasn't carrying another weapon, unless it was tucked in his waistband under his shirt. Raph wasn't big on carrying since he was usually surrounded by people who did, but today Raph was alone. It's possible he had a bodyguard out front, maybe waiting in the car, but Gabe felt he could do what he had planned either way.

Raph picked up a newspaper from one of the chairs for waiting and sat in the barber chair.

Gabe took his own nine-millimeter pistol out of his waist holster and removed his hat and sunglasses. He stepped out of the dark hallway.

"Raph. It's been a long time," Gabe said, aiming the pistol at Raph.

Raph turned and recognized Gabe right away, despite the changes in his appearance. Raph turned white when he saw the gun pointed at him.

"Gabe?" he said, as if feigning not to recognize him.

"Yep, it's me, old buddy. Now I want you to listen very carefully. I want you to slowly untuck your shirt."

Raph complied, and it was clear he was not carrying.

"I noticed you sent some guys to find me in the apartment I was borrowing," Gabe said. "It was Phil and Denny, I believe."

"Yeah. I sent them to talk to you and find out what you're up to."

"I guess that's why they beat up and killed my friend."

"They just wanted to talk. Your friend pulled a gun and they had to respond," Raph said. "We wanted you to know that we're willing to let bygones be bygones if you stay out of our neighborhood and don't compete with us."

Gabe moved sideways to the coat rack, keeping his gun aimed at Raph. He reached into the right pocket of Raph's jacket and pulled out a small pistol. In a quick motion, Gabe pushed the button on the side of the gun to release the magazine and racked the slide to remove the bullet in the chamber. Gabe laid the gun down on one of the chairs.

"If that's the way you feel, why are you trying so hard to kill me?" Gabe asked.

"We weren't, but maybe we should. You broke my sister's heart. You ratted out my father, and you came back like nothing happened," Raph said, gaining a little composure. "And now you're pointing a gun at me. You've shown nothing but disrespect for my family. Do you think Maria will forgive you if you kill her brother?"

"Do you think Maria will forgive you after you betrayed her to the Carbone family? Because Hank Maranzano told me what you did."

"Don't believe anything that son of a bitch tells you," Raph said, shaking his head.

"I do believe it, and I think you also tipped off the FBI that the Carbones were following Maria and me to the cabin. Did you think they wouldn't arrest me when they found us? I almost died protecting your sister," Gabe said with an icy stare. "Maybe it was one big grand plan. You knew I would get caught and testify against your father, and that when he went to prison, you would become boss."

"You're crazy. So why don't you just do what you came here to do and get it over with?"

"You know I had no choice about testifying. They could have put your father away even without my testimony. I just made it easier. What would you have done? Would you have gone to prison until you're an old man or would you have made a deal with the government?"

"You know the rules, Gabe. Anyone who breaks the code of silence needs to pay with their life."

"Well, at least you're finally being honest with me. The only thing is, when they got my computer, the code of silence became irrelevant because they had what they needed."

"You make it sound so simple. Now why don't you get on with it?"

"I'm proposing a new deal. You give me your word that you'll call off your goons and stop trying to kill me and I'll let you go. I promise I'll stay out of this neighborhood. I won't compete with you, and you won't see me again."

"What about Maria?" Raph asked. "You gonna promise you'll keep away from her as well?"

"I can't make that promise. But you have my word on the rest. You won't see me around here again. Oh, and I want *you* to promise you won't do anything to hurt Maria.

"I was going to say the same thing to you. If you hurt her in any way, the deal is off."

"Don't worry. She's probably going to marry that guy she's been seeing anyway. So do we have a deal?"

"Yeah, we do," Raph said, pinching his lips together.

"Now I just need to take some precautions. Keep still for a minute." Gabe pulled a roll of duct tape out a bag he had laid by the wall. He pulled out a long length and wrapped it around Raph, taping him to the barber chair. The tape wouldn't hold him long, but it would give Gabe a chance to sneak out the back and get away.

"Is this really necessary?" Raph asked.

"Yeah, it is. Well Raph, it's been a pleasure doing business with you. And I really am sorry about your mother. I considered her a friend when I worked with you guys."

Raph didn't answer, but gave Gabe an evil stare as he picked up his bag and slipped out the back.

Just then, Tony the barber came in the front door of the shop holding a small pizza-size box.

"What the hell?"

"Where were you?" Raph asked as Tony helped extricate him from the duct tape.

"The guy who was here said he was an old friend of yours and wanted to surprise you. He asked me to pick up some cannoli for you at the bakery," Tony explained.

"Don't ever listen to anyone who wants to surprise me, or even see me. You let me handle all my visitors," Raph said angrily.

"I'm sorry. They guy looked sincere, and he kind of looked familiar."

"You could have gotten me killed."

"I'm really sorry, boss," Tony said, starting to tremble. He didn't know all the details of Raph's business, but he knew it was never a good idea to get on the bad side of the D'Angelo family. Tony got the last of the duct tape off and Raph stood up abruptly.

"You're not going to tell anyone about this little episode, you got that? I mean no one. Not a word about the visitor or me being taped up here. If I find out you leaked this, you'll regret it," Raph said and handed Tony two twenty-dollar bills.

"You don't want a haircut?"

"Put me down for next week." Raph walked out and slammed the door. On the street, he called for his driver, who had parked around the block. As he got in the car, he called Gus Nasuti.

"Morning, boss. You done with your haircut already?" Gus asked.

"No. There was a change of plans. I saw Rossi this morning and he's in the neighborhood. I want you to put the word out to as many as possible to be on the lookout for him. Have a few cars patrol the area. Rossi was on foot when he left me."

"He left you? What happened?"

"I'll explain when I see you. Can you and Phil meet me at the clubhouse?"

"Yeah. We'll see you in a few," Gus said. "I'll put the word out right away, like you asked."

♦ ♦ ♦

A few minutes before eleven, Raph stood in the main meeting room at the clubhouse with Gus and Phil. He poured himself a glass of bourbon from the bar despite the early hour and sat down. Gus and Phil had cups of coffee.

"He came right into the barber shop and pulled a gun on me," Raph said.

"Was the barber there?" Gus asked with a puzzled look on his face.

"No. Rossi paid him to go and get some cannoli down the street. I was alone when I went in, and he stepped out of the back room." Raph neglected to add the detail about being taped to the chair.

"How'd you manage to escape alive?" Phil asked.

"He told me he'd let me go if I called off the hit, and I said okay," Raph said, draining his drink and getting up for a refill at the table behind him.

"So, Gabe's in the clear now?" Gus asked, raising his eyebrows.

"Hell no! Nobody who breaks our code of silence and then pulls a gun on me is off the hook. I said what I had to say to get out of there. Now, why don't you guys explain to me why you haven't found him yet."

"We been looking around the clock boss. You know how it is with Rossi, he's good at hiding. But he can't hide forever."

"Well, I want you guys to find him, and I mean now. It's embarrassing we can't track down someone who's obviously in the area," Raph said as beads of sweat began to form on his face. "If he can get that close to me, none of us is safe."

"As a matter of fact," Phil said, "I was just explaining a little plan I have to Gus. I was going to surprise you with it by bringing Gabe in, but under the circumstances, I'd like to fill you in."

"I'm all ears," Raph said as his voice began to reflect that he had just downed two large glasses of bourbon.

"Well, the first time we found Gabe, it was by following your sister Maria, right?"

"I don't think that will work this time. She's smart enough not to lead us right to him again."

"Yeah, but if she's helping him, and we know she's done that already, she may know where he is."

"If you think I'm going to let you work my sister over to get information, you're wrong. At least for now. I told you guys before that you don't touch her."

"We won't have to. Let me explain."

CHAPTER 32

Later that evening, after Brian had finished washing the dishes and put them away, he poured a glass of pinot grigio and sat on the couch in his small family room. He flicked on the local news affiliate and sat on the sofa to watch the headlines before checking out the latest movie offerings on Netflix. In a little while, he would give Maria a call to see how she was doing, as he did most nights that he wasn't with her. Focused on the television, he didn't hear the two large men with black face masks sneaking up behind him. They didn't even need to pick his lock; his front door was unlocked, as Brian's concerns about the mysterious black SUV had faded based on Maria's assurances. The larger of the two intruders held in his hands a garrot made of thick, soft rope, which he silently slipped over Brian's head and pulled tight. Brian let out a scream and instinctively reached for his neck, but he couldn't get his fingers under the rope. As Brian struggled to stand up, the man holding the garrot pulled backward and he fell back onto the couch. No longer able to scream, Brian struggled one final time. The intruder tightened the rope around Brian's neck just long enough for him to pass out and slump down on the couch.

"Are there any chairs with armrests?" asked the intruder with the garrot.

"In the dining room," said the other. "I'll bring one in here," He walked over and pulled the chair from the head of the small dining room table into the family room.

"Thanks, Danny."

"You want the head cover, Leo?"

"Yeah, set it right here on the couch,"

Danny reached into a duffle bag and pulled out a black cloth bag and a roll of duct tape. "Let's get him taped up."

They shifted Brian onto the chair and held him upright as they wrapped lengths of tape around his chest and the back of the chair. They wrapped tape around Brian's arms, securing them to the arms of the chair, then taped his ankles to the front legs of the chair.

As Brian began to come to, he took several rapid deep breaths. His eyes opened with a look of terror as he struggled against the tape on his arms.

"Who are you and what do you want?" Brian shouted.

Leo reached around and pulled out a compact Glock pistol that had been tucked under his belt. "Shut the hell up!" he yelled.

Brian continued to breathe rapidly and was now shifting back and forth as if to loosen the tape. "What do you want?" he shouted again.

Leo pistol-whipped Brian across the face, leaving him with a gash on his cheek and a bloody nose. "Don't speak until we tell you to!"

"I'm just a schoolteacher. I don't have much, but take what you want. My wallet is on the kitchen counter," Brian said, gaining a little composure.

"I said shut up!" Leo shouted as he smacked Brian hard in the face with his gloved hand. This time he hit lower and cut Brian's lip open. The nosebleed and the cut lip made Brian's face look like a bloody mess.

"I'm going to ask you something, so I want you to listen carefully. Do you know where Gabriel Rossi is hiding? Your girlfriend has been helping him, and I think she told you where he is. If you want to wake up tomorrow morning, you'd better tell me the truth."

"I have no idea where he is. I've never even met the guy," Brian replied, struggling to speak with the wounds on his face.

Leo slapped Brian hard again. "I said you need to tell us where he is!"

"You want me to get the pliers?" Danny asked.

"Yeah. You hear that, Mr. Murphy? We got a pair of pliers and we're going to start pulling things off your body." Leo held up the pair of pliers that Danny had handed him. "Do you like your fingers, Mr. Murphy? First we break them with these, and then they're easy to pull off."

"No! I said I don't know. I don't know and I don't care. You can catch Gabe and do whatever you want to him for all I care. I have no idea where he is!"

Leo smashed the pliers down on Brian's hand, hard enough to cause pain without breaking any bones.

Brian screamed. "No! Please don't. I'll do anything you want, I just don't know where Gabe is!"

Leo picked up the black bag off the couch and put it over Brian's head.

"No! no! Please no more. I wish I knew where he is!"

"Just shut up unless you want us to hurt you more," Leo said as he signaled to Danny to follow him out to the kitchen.

"I don't think he knows anything, Leo," Danny whispered, wiping the sweat off his brow.

Leo pulled out his phone and dialed. "I think we're ready, Phil. Is everything in place?"

"Yeah. We're parked outside her house. How bad is the guy hurt?"

"We roughed him up a little. He looks a lot worse than he is. He's got some bruises and cuts on his face. I think it'll work."

"Good. We'll call you in a few," Phil said and hung up.

◆　◆　◆

Phil Morino rang the doorbell to Maria's townhouse. She had just settled in to work on her lesson plans.

"Ms. D'Angelo?" Phil said when she opened the door.

"Yes, may I help you?" Maria asked.

"I think we met at your brother's home about a week ago. I have something I'd like to talk to you about. I won't take up much of your time."

"What's this about?" she said with anger in her voice. She couldn't imagine what Phil Morino would want with her, and after hearing he may have been involved in a murder, she really wanted nothing to do with him.

"I'll only take a few minutes. Why don't I come in and explain it to you?"

Maria felt nervous about the whole situation, but she knew Phil was one of Raph's top men and felt confident her brother would not harm her. Suddenly, she had an idea.

"Okay, can you give me a second? I just need to take care of something."

Maria left Phil in the doorway and walked into her small living room. It sounded to him like she was turning lights on, then she returned to the foyer. "Come in and have a seat. Can I offer you a cup of coffee?" she asked, attempting to appear calm. She directed Phil to sit on a sofa and she sat on a chair to the side of the room.

"No thanks, I'm good."

"Maria, can I call you that?" She nodded. "We understand you've had some contact with Gabriel Rossi. Your brother is concerned since Mr. Rossi is a dangerous man."

Maria stared at Phil expressionless and didn't answer.

"I assume you know where to locate him? Your brother would like to speak to him, and Mr. Rossi hasn't told anyone where he is."

"Well, I suppose there's a reason he hasn't told anyone. I don't think he feels safe right now."

"Maria, you really need to tell me where he is so we can protect you from him," Phil said, staring intently at her. "Don't let him deceive you."

"I can't say where he is right now," she said with a sigh. "And I don't need protection from Gabe."

"Maria, I need to show you something and I'm afraid it will be disturbing to you. Gabe sent us a photo of someone. I believe you know him quite well. Here's what he sent us about an hour ago." Phil took out his phone and showed her a picture of Brian, strapped to the chair with a bloodied face.

"What??" she shrieked, reaching for Phil's phone. "Where is he, and what have you done to him?"

"He's alive, but Gabe has threatened to kill him if we don't meet his demands," Phil said without emotion.

"You bastards! Gabe wouldn't do that. You have Brian and you've hurt him badly! I'm calling the police!"

"I don't recommend that. If you give us an address for Gabe, we'll make sure Brian is not hurt any further," he answered, admitting to the charade.

"Get out of my house!" Mara shouted.

"If you care at all for Mr. Murphy, you'll give me an address. If you don't, he's going to die."

"If I give you the address, you'll release Brian immediately?"

"Nothing further will happen to Brian if you give us a good address and your phone. We'll send it back to you after we find Rossi."

"First you need to prove to me that Brian is still alive."

"He's alive, I promise. Just hold on a second," He pulled out an iPhone and dialed a number for a Facetime call. "Okay, show us Brian," Phil said as he placed the phone in front of Maria so she could see the screen. Maria heard some mumbling on the other end as she saw a black hood pulled from Brian's bloodied face. One eye was swollen shut, and blood was flowing from Brian's nose.

Maria took one look and screamed. "You bastards! Let him go right now!"

"Do you want to say something to your beloved Maria?" Phil asked Brian loud enough for Maria to hear.

Brian's cut, swollen lip made it hard for him to speak. "Jus' … Jus' give 'em what they want," he managed to get out before someone replaced the black bag over his head.

"Okay, okay, I'll give you an address. Here's my phone. Take it." Maria got up and walked to a secretary desk in the hallway. She opened a small notebook and read the address to Phil.

"Let me take a picture of that," he said, and Maria handed him the notebook open to the page with the address of Julie's listing.

"Now get out! You are vile, evil people!" Maria shouted.

"I can't promise anything if this isn't a good address."

"It's good, now get out!"

As Phil walked out and shut the door, Maria stood hyperventilating. She literally fell back on the couch and started to pray out loud. "Please God, let Brian be okay." Then she struggled to get up and ran upstairs to her bedroom. She pulled the burner phone out from under the mattress where she had hidden it and dialed 911.

"Maple Grove Emergency Services."

"There's been a break-in at five twenty-one Inman Terrace in Maple Grove. I believe someone is badly hurt."

"Could you give me your name?"

"Maria D'Angelo."

"Are you there at the scene, ma'am?"

"No, one of the people who broke in just threatened me."

"I'm sorry ma'am, how did they threaten you if you're not at the scene?"

"Please just get an ambulance over there. Brian Murphy lives there and they hurt him bad. I'll be there in a few minutes and explain."

"Don't worry ma'am. May I have your home address?"

Maria gave the information and hung up. She almost fainted when she tried to get up from the bed, so she sat back down and breathed deeply for a moment before rushing downstairs to look for her car keys. When they weren't on her kitchen table, she began gasping for air and felt a tightness in her chest. She nearly fainted again and sat down on her sofa, trying to breathe deeply. When she was able to get up, she saw the keys on her kitchen counter. She got up to grab them, then paused.

"Oh no!" she said, remembering she needed to call Gabe. She dialed the number she had memorized.

"Maria," Gabe said when he picked up.

"You need to get out of the house. They know where you are. Hurry, please. They're coming."

"Who's coming?"

"Raph's people. They're coming for you. Right now. I'm so sorry."

"How did they find out?"

"They have Brian. They hurt him and they were going to kill them if I didn't give them the address."

"Don't worry, Maria. I'll be out of here in a minute. Don't apologize. I know how these people operate and I should have seen this coming."

"There's more to tell, but I need to get to Brian's house. An ambulance is on its way."

"Okay. Don't worry about me. Go take care of Brian. I'll be fine."

"Call me when you get to a safe place, and I'll tell you more."

Maria took a moment to calm herself. As she whispered a prayer for Brian, she started to realize the depth of her attachment to him. Whatever feelings she might have for Gabe, she knew that Brian was her man now. She grabbed a cardigan and her purse and keys and left for Brian's house. She knew she was in a panic, so she tried her best to drive carefully, obeying the speed limits. When she turned on to Brian's street, she saw police cars and an ambulance parked in front of his house. Several bystanders stood on the sidewalk across the street, obviously curious as to what was going on with the young schoolteacher. Maria pulled over, jumped out of the car, and ran across Brian's front lawn.

A police officer was standing in front of the door. "I'm sorry ma'am, but you can't come in. This is a crime scene and the medical technicians are taking care of the man who lives here."

"The man who lives here is Brian Murphy. He's my fiancée," she said, stretching the truth to see if she could get closer. "And I'm the one who called nine one one."

"Still can't let you in right now. I'll have someone come speak to you," he said as he turned and entered the house.

A moment later, a short Black woman in a police uniform stepped out. "Are you the woman who called this in?"

"Yes. I'm Maria D'Angelo. I'm a very close friend of Brian Murphy, the victim. Is he okay?"

"He's conscious and talking to us, but we're gonna take him to Abington Hospital so they can check him out. I'm Sergeant Marjorie Stile and I'm the officer in charge here. Now do I understand correctly that you weren't here when the intruders came?"

"That's right."

"So did Mr. Murphy call you for help?"

"No. Someone came to my townhouse. I live on Mill Avenue. They told me someone had Brian captive, but I'm sure the one who visited me was responsible. That is, he had someone else come here to attack Brian."

"Now slow down. I'm not sure I understand. You say 'they' came. Who are 'they'?"

"It was a man. I believe his name was Phil. I'm having trouble remembering his last name," Maria said truthfully.

"And this man, Phil, threatened you? What did he say?"

"He wanted some information, and he showed me a picture of Brian, who's my boyfriend. He said if I gave him the information, they wouldn't hurt him," Maria started to cry.

"What information was this Phil looking for?" the sergeant asked.

Maria knew she was getting into an area of questioning that might be dangerous for Gabe. As far as she knew, the police and the FBI were still looking for him. She didn't want to help them find Gabe, and she knew she was at risk of being an accessory if it came out she had helped him hide. Maria put her head in her hands and began to hyperventilate. "I'm not feeling well. I don't think I can talk now," she said.

Luckily for Maria, the emergency medical technicians began to wheel Brian out on a stretcher to a waiting ambulance, and one of the policemen came out of the house and called for Sergeant Stiles.

"I've got to go to the hospital with Mr. Murphy, but we need to talk more. Can you give me a phone number?"

Maria gave her number and the sergeant began to walk away. Maria remembered Phil took her phone and that the sergeant would have trouble reaching her without it. But she had given her street address to the emergency operator, so they'd be able to find her. At least she could avoid talking for now. As they wheeled Brian by, he looked in her direction, expressionless.

"Brian. Are you okay?"

Brian didn't answer and looked the other way.

"I'm so sorry!" Maria shouted, trying to get Brian's attention. As they picked up the gurney to slide it into the ambulance, Maria shouted again. "I'll come to the hospital soon." Maria knew she wouldn't be able to see Brian while the doctors were checking him out. Then there were the police who would be hovering over him, at least for a while. She wanted to avoid them for now if possible. She was also worried about Gabe. *Would he make it out of the house all right?* Gabe was smart and resourceful. He'd find a way to keep one step ahead of his pursuers and hopefully call her soon from a safe location. Maria walked to her car, sat inside, and put her head in her hands. The hospital was about ten minutes away, but she decided to stop at church, which was just a few minutes away, to light a candle for Brian and offer prayers.

CHAPTER 33

Phil Morino left Maria's home quickly because he knew either Maria or Brian would contact the police. It was nearly a half hour drive to the address Maria had given him. Assuming she even gave the correct address, that was plenty of time for Gabe to pick up and leave if Maria was able to get word to him. He called Denny, who was closer, to get over to the address and see if he could intercept Gabe. Phil asked some other soldiers to patrol the streets as well. Denny was waiting out front when Phil arrived. He had been patrolling the area with Tony Marianni driving.

"I don't think he's in there," Denny said. "No one has come out the front or the back, and there's no sign of life.

"When did you get here?"

"I was here in ten minutes. If Gabe got away, he must have been packed and ready to go."

"Anybody else see anything?"

"No. We got three cars driving around the area, and no one's reported seeing Rossi."

"Well, let's head in and see for ourselves," Phil said as the two approached the front door. They both had noticed the "For Sale" sign out front. "Be careful, we don't know if we got a good address, and we don't know if anyone is home. They tried the door and it wasn't locked. Phil and Denny pulled their pistols and entered cautiously, clearing the rooms on the ground floor.

Denny went upstairs. A moment later, he shouted to Phil, "All clear up here. Looks like somebody slept in the bed in the big bedroom."

Phil noticed a card in an envelope on the dining room table with writing on the outside that said, "Please read this message to Raph." Phil opened the envelope and read the note inside: "What happened to our agreement?" It was signed "Gabe."

"Gabe was definitely here," Phil said, holding up the note.

"You gonna call the boss?" Denny asked.

"I guess I have to." Phil scowled. "Before I do, I wonder how Gabe found this place? I'm sure he didn't just pick a house with a for sale sign at random," he said, scratching is chin. "Wait a minute," he said, walking toward the front door. "There's somebody named 'Julie Ryan' on the sign. I wonder if she was involved in this."

"If she was involved, maybe she found another location for Gabe to use," Denny said.

"Let's get somebody working on this. Call the clubhouse and see if one of those computer whizzes can find out more about this woman," Phil pulled out his phone and found their location on Google Maps. "Take a look at this. If you had to escape quickly, where would you go?" he asked.

"It would depend on whether I had a car or not. If I had a car, I'd head in almost any direction to get out of here. Maybe not toward Chestnut Hill, where Raph is located, but it wouldn't be hard to get away. If I was on foot or on a bike, I might head over to the park to the west. It looks like a ten- or fifteen-minute walk and you could disappear into the trails,"

"Maybe so. What about train stations?"

"Yeah, there's a SEPTA station about the same distance. But if a lot of people were looking for me, I'd probably avoid the train station,"

"Let's get some guys at the train station right away, and we'll go to the park. Let me send a quick text to Raph first, then we'll head over."

CHAPTER 34

When Maria looked at her watch, she was surprised to see that she had been kneeling in the church praying for almost an hour. It was time to go to the hospital. Ten minutes later, she was cruising around the hospital looking for a parking space. She wanted to avoid the parking garage because she didn't know if the police would be watching, so she drove a couple of blocks down a residential street to find a spot. Then she walked around to the front entrance where a guard copied her drivers' license, took a photo of her, and handed her a visitor sticker with her picture on it to be placed on her blouse.

Maria approached the information desk. "Could you tell me what room Brian Murphy is in please?" she asked, not knowing if Brian had been admitted or was still in the emergency room.

"Was he in the emergency room?" the attendant asked.

"He came in by ambulance, so probably."

"He's not admitted, so I suggest you try the ER."

After the attendant gave a complicated series of directions involving hallways and elevators, Maria headed to the ER.

When Maria finally reached the doorway to the ER, she stopped at another reception desk.

"I'm looking for Brian Murphy. Is he still here?"

"Yes he is. Are you a relative?" the attendant asked.

"I'm his fiancée."

"Go down corridor A and he's in room twelve." The attendant hit a button that unlocked and automatically opened the doors.

"Are the police still with him? I don't want to interrupt."

"They just left."

Maria rushed down the corridor to Room 12, which was just a bay surrounded by curtains. There was a nurse typing at a computer on a raised cart. When Maria turned the corner, she was shocked. Brian had stitches on his cheek and lip and a large bandage across his face, covering his nose.

"Brian?" she said quietly.

He opened his eyes and greeted her with a blank stare.

"How are you, darling?" she said, using a word she rarely used.

"Well, you can pretty much see for yourself," he answered in a hoarse voice.

"I mean, are you okay? Are they going to let you go home?"

"They're sending me down for a CT scan to make sure I don't have a concussion, since I felt a little dizzy coming in."

"Did the doctor tell you anything?" she asked.

"No, other than that I needed stitches, I have a broken tooth and a broken nose. They'll probably keep me overnight to make sure I'm okay."

"I'm so sorry this happened to you," she said, putting her hand on Brian's hand.

"I told you not to get involved." Brian moved his hand out from under Maria's and looked at her with sternly.

"What do you mean?"

"You know exactly what I mean. They came after me because you've been helping Gabe run from your brother. It makes me wonder if you've really gotten over him." Brian grimaced from the throbbing pain of the stitches in his lip. "Of course, I'm the one who suffered the consequences of all this," he said.

"Brian I am over Gabe and I'm with you now! I've never heard of them going after family member or their friends." Maria took a breath and began to weep. "I'd never do anything if I thought they might hurt you."

"Well, they did. Your brother's thugs broke into my house. I didn't even hear them come in. I was just watching TV and the next thing I know I'm being strangled with a rope until I pass out. Can you imagine how terrifying that was? When I woke up I was taped to a chair, and they were asking me if I knew where Gabe was."

"I'm so sorry, Brian."

Brian wasn't finished. "They came at me was because they know you're that connected to me, so they naturally assumed we talk about things and that maybe you told me where Gabe was hiding. When I didn't know anything, they sent you the picture they took of me all banged up and bloody to scare you into talking."

Maria looked down as tears formed in her eyes. "Brian, I'm so, so sorry. How can you ever forgive me?"

"In case you're wondering, I didn't say anything to the police about you helping Gabe, but I did tell them the thugs asked me if I knew where Gabe was. Then they asked me why anyone would think I knew something."

Maria took a tissue out of her purse and wiped her eyes. "So what did you say?"

"I said I didn't know but that I've been dating Maria D'Angelo and she's got a brother who's involved with some bad stuff in Philadelphia. I'm sure they knew who your brother is. If they didn't, they'll figure it out soon."

"Brian, I feel so awful about what happened. I don't think Gabe has done anything wrong, at least nothing since he left witness protection. Was it wrong for me to help someone who doesn't deserve what's happening to him?" She wiped her tears again. "I had no idea they'd do anything to you."

"Gabe was able to walk away from serious felony charges with a slap on the wrist. I'm sure he can get out of the current trouble he's in. Didn't you say that all he had to do was leave town?" Brian asked.

"I said he should leave town to get away from this, but I don't know for sure if that will solve all his problems."

"Well, I don't want them to be my problems anymore. As I said, maybe deep down, you're not really over Gabe," Brian said.

"Brian, I am over Gabe and it hurts me that you think that. And Gabe's problems aren't your problems."

"Well, if they're not my problems, why am I in the hospital?"

"Brian, all I can say is how shattered I am about this. Are you worried they'll come after you again? Because if you are, I will make sure they don't," Maria said.

"You had no idea they'd come after me this time. How can you make sure?"

"Maybe I don't have a lot of pull with Raph, but I think I can get him to stay away from you."

"Really? Your pull didn't do me much good so far."

Maria wiped her eyes with her sleeve. "Brian, if there's anything I can do for you, just say so. Do you want me to pick you up and take you home tomorrow?"

"My brother is driving down from Reading to help me. He'll drive me home and he'll stay a few days. Right now I need some space between me and the D'Angelo family."

"Does that include me?" she asked, putting her tissue down and looking at Brian.

"I think you know what I mean."

"Okay then, if that's what you want," she said, wiping a tear from her eye. "Please let me know how you're doing and if there's anything I can do." Maria got up from her seat. She stood by the bed and kissed Brian's forehead. He had no reaction, just stared straight ahead. Maria left the room.

When she got back to her car, Maria began to weep. She didn't remember being this heartbroken in her life. Brian was a good man. He had been a perfect gentleman since they started their relationship almost three years ago, and he had obviously loved her. She couldn't bear to think of the trauma he had experienced, and it was all because of his relationship with her. She wanted to be with him, to hug and comfort him, but she doubted he'd even answer her phone calls now. *What if I've lost him forever?*

CHAPTER 35

After going through the house, Denny left Tony and hopped in Phil's vehicle. Phil's phone rang just as they were leaving. It was Raph.

"What's going on? You were supposed to call me."

"I know, but things are movin' fast right now," Phil replied.

"Fast or slow, just tell me what's happening," Raph said, sounding impatient.

"The girl, I mean your sister, gave us the right address. It's a house in Germantown that no one is living in because it's for sale. Denny got there about ten minutes after she told us the address and Rossi was already gone. He left a note that said, 'What happened to our agreement?' I don't know how he got tipped off. We took your sister's phone."

"Don't insult my intelligence. Gabe probably gave her a burner phone at some point when she started helping him. What I'm wondering is how they found an empty house that was for sale. Did they get a realtor to help them?"

"There was a sign out front with the agent's name. Denny, do you remember the name? He says the agent is Julie Ryan."

"Wait a minute. I think that's the girl who got kicked out of the convent when Maria was there. My father got her a job working at one of Joey's restaurants," Raph said. "She must be returning the favor to Maria."

"We can run her down later," Phil replied. "Gabe couldn't have gotten too far since he's on foot and left the house just a few minutes ago. I got cars patrolling the area, and we had a hunch he might be headed to the park just west of here. We're headed there now."

"Let me know what you find," Raph said. "No more mistakes. Gabe is making us look like idiots."

No sooner had Phil ended the call than the park entrance came into sight. There was a spot for cars to pull over at the trailhead.

"Look, there's a guy with a backpack up ahead. I can't tell for sure, but it sure looks like it could be Gabe," Denny said, pointing.

"There's a pair of binoculars in the glove compartment. Hand 'em to me," Phil said as he stopped the car. Phil grabbed the binoculars and looked at the man walking into the park. Just then, the man looked behind him, and saw the SUV with Phil and Denny in it.

"It's him!" Phil said. "He's starting to run. Let's get this bastard!"

The two men got out and started running. They continued past a sign explaining the trail system and began running faster on the packed gravel trail, which had thick vegetation on both sides and towering trees above. About a hundred feet ahead of them, the trail wound to the left.

"Let's go!" Phil said, breathing heavily. "We gotta see what's around that corner."

Phil wasn't used to running, but he couldn't let Gabe get away again. When they reached the bend in the trail, they saw a fork split the trail in two directions. "Shit," Phil said. "I think we gotta split up. You go to the right and I'll go to the left. Keep your gun ready in case he's luring us into an ambush."

"Got it," Denny said. "How far should I go?"

"Just keep going until you're sure he isn't ahead of you. Call me in fifteen minutes or if you find him. I'll do the same."

The two men headed down the paths.

◆ ◆ ◆

Gabe was crouching in the bushes as he watched Phil and Denny run by. He saw them slow down as they approached the fork in the trail and figured they might split up. They did. He waited a minute or so, then quietly moved through the trees toward the park entrance. When he got there, he stepped out onto the trail and looked back. There was no sign of Phil or Denny. Gabe trotted down to the black GMC Denali his pursuers had hurriedly left on the roadside. He tried the door and it was unlocked, but the keys were gone. Getting in, he pulled out a small toolkit from his backpack and began working under the dashboard.

It took less than a minute for Gabe to start the vehicle. He made a u-turn and drove east. When he arrived at Germantown Avenue, he turned north toward Chestnut Hill. Before he got there, he called for an Uber to meet him on a corner in about fifteen minutes. Gabe drove the SUV to Raph's house and parked the car on the street just out of sight from the front door. Gabe quickly scribbled a note that read, "Raph: I kept my end of our agreement. It's time to keep yours. I mean you no harm. Gabe."

Knowing he was taking a big risk, Gabe got out of the SUV, quietly closed the door, and trotted down the street back to Germantown Avenue. As far as he could tell, no one saw him. When he got to the corner, he saw the Uber he had called and got in. He had booked a ride to an address near Broad and Olney in North Philadelphia. When they arrived, he got out and walked toward an auto repair shop with a sign that read, "Jimmy Lee Auto Repair." Gabe knew the shop doubled as a chop shop to break down and sell parts from stolen cars. The D'Angelo family did not do business with Jimmy Lee; they rarely worked with minority-owned businesses. Gabe had gone to Jimmy to buy some hard-to-find parts for D'Angelo family's vehicles, and the two had become friendly acquaintances. Since Jimmy had no loyalty to the D'Angelo family, Gabe figured he could trust Jimmy to keep quiet about the present dealings.

When Gabe got out of the Uber, a group of Black teens on the corner stared at him; it was unusual for someone to venture into the neighborhood after dark. Gabe ordinarily didn't fear such situations, but he was carrying a large stash of cash in his duffle bag. Gabe walked briskly into the shop.

"Is Jimmy around?" Gabe asked a young man working on a car on a lift.

"Who's askin'?"

"Tell him it's Gabe Rossi,"

The young man disappeared around the corner while Gabe cooled his heels. In a moment he returned. "C'mon back," he said, and Gabe followed into a small office with a cluttered desk and various posters for automotive products on the walls. There were piles of manuals and car parts on various tables and shelves around the edges of the room. A bouquet of motor oil and grease permeated the air.

"So, what brings my favorite fugitive around?" Jimmy said with a big smile on his face.

"So you know about my situation?" Gabe asked.

"Who doesn't? I'm assuming this ain't just a social call."

"I need some wheels. Nothing fancy, just a way to get around for a while."

"If you got money, I might have something. It definitely ain't fancy, but you won't stand out, which I assume is what you want."

"Sounds like what I need," Gabe said. "And I can pay cash for it."

"It's a Honda Civic, about six years old, runs well. Dark gray. There's a lot of them driving around just like this one, so you'll blend right in. You can adjust the seat if it's a tight fit for you."

"Sounds good," Gabe said. "I assume our dealings here will stay between us?" He looked Jimmy in the eye.

"I don't owe nothin' to the D'Angelos, and I definitely don't owe nothin' to the police. So yeah. This will be our little secret. The car's from New Jersey. Owner just went into a nursing home so nobody's lookin' for it. Let me have Nate bring it around."

Jimmy walked to the door and shouted to Nate, the man Gabe had encountered, to bring the Honda around front. Gabe had worked on cars when he was younger and knew a lot about them. When he saw the car and looked under the hood, it appeared to be clean and in good shape.

"It'll be five bills. It's worth more 'n that but I'll give you that price for old times' sake."

Gabe reached into his duffle, counted out five thousand dollars, and laid the cash on Jimmy's table. "Thanks, Jimmy. I owe you for this one."

"Not at all, Gabe. Nice doin' business with you again. Be careful carrying that much money around a neighborhood like this at night," Jimmy said with a smirk.

Gabe got in the car and was driving toward the Schuylkill Expressway to get out of the city when he thought of Maria, so he picked up one of his burner phones and dialed.

Maria picked up on the third ring. "Gabe?" she asked hesitatingly.

"It's me," he said. "I'm okay. I'm driving out of the city."

"You got a car?"

"Yeah. Long story. You told me to call you when I was in a safe spot. I'm pretty safe now since I'm driving a car they don't know about. I'm on the expressway heading out of the city. Are you home?"

"No. I'm sitting in my car outside Abington Hospital. I just went to see Brian."

"Is he okay?"

"I think so. He's pretty banged up though," she said as she began to lose composure. "He blames me for what happened to him."

"I'm so sorry, Maria. It's my fault. I shouldn't have dragged you into this."

"No," Maria said. "It's my brother's fault and you don't deserve to die for anything you've done. As far as I'm concerned, you've made some mistakes, but you've paid your dues and I want to help you."

"I can't tell you how much it means to hear you say that," Gabe said, his voice thick with emotion. "I think you said there was more to tell."

"When I found out Raph knew I was helping you, I was worried his men might break into my house. So I got a little wall outlet video camera. After my father went to prison, I found out that my parents had these all around their home, so I borrowed one."

"What did you record?"

"I got a recording of Phil Morino threatening me. Well, threatening to kill Brian if I didn't give him your address."

"You got Phil threatening you and Brian? That's incredible! This could change everything. But Maria, you need to be very careful. Don't tell anyone you have this or you won't be safe."

"So what should I do?"

"Put the SD card it's recorded on in a safe place. When we can meet, I'll make a copy of it on my laptop. Wait, can you put it on your computer?"

"I'll try. If I can't, I'm sure someone at school can help me. They won't have to see what's on the video, will they?"

"No. If I give you an email address, can you send it to me?"

"Yes. If I can put it on my computer. But what if the FBI is watching?" Maria asked.

"I don't care so much if the FBI finds it. What I'm worried about is your brother. If he gets wind you have this, you could be in real danger."

"Okay, what's the email address?"

Gabe gave her an address that had no trace of his name but consisted of random numbers and letters and the term "AJAXX.com. "Don't worry," Gabe said. "If you use that address, no one will be able to trace it back to you or me. Don't leave the video on your computer.

Delete it and the email. Just keep a copy of it on the SD card and put it in a safe place."

"Got it. I'll get this done tomorrow."

"Maria, thanks so much for this. This could be a game changer," Gabe said.

"Where are you going to stay now?" Maria asked.

"I'll find a place to crash tonight. After that, I'll figure something out."

"I might have an idea."

"Maria, I'm very thankful for your help, but I've already put you in enough danger. Let's talk tomorrow. Call me when you get a chance. Oh, you should let your realtor friend know I'm not there, and I think you should warn her that some people might be asking about me."

"She doesn't know anything other than I needed a place for a friend to crash for a few days, and that's what she would tell them." Maria said.

"I'm sure you're right. Raph's not going to waste time on her," Gabe said.

"So be careful yourself Gabe and I'll call you tomorrow morning."

CHAPTER 36

Phil ran along the trail until he got tired, then began to walk. It was growing dark, and he hadn't heard from Denny. Phil pulled out his phone and saw that he could still get a signal in the park. He dialed.

"Yeah," Denny answered.

"You were supposed to call me. See anything?"

"No. You?"

"Nothin'. Where are you?"

"I'm not sure. It's easy to get lost on these trails. It's getting dark and nobody is around."

"You're lost?

"Well, I'm not sure where I am."

"What the hell, Denny! Can't you try walking back to where we split up?"

"I'll try," Denny said.

◆　◆　◆

After a half hour of looking, Phil found Denny, and they made their way back to the park entrance.

"Where's the car? Didn't we leave it right over there?" Phil asked impatiently, pointing to a spot about seventy-five feet away.

"Yeah. You don't think it was stolen, do you?"

"I've got the key, but we were in a hurry and I don't know if I locked it."

"But without the key, you can't start the newer cars, can you?" Denny asked.

"If anyone could figure out how to start it, I'm sure Gabe could." Phil began to shake his head. "Shit! Now I've got to call for a ride."

"You gonna call the boss?"

"No, not yet," Phil pulled out his phone and called Tony Marianni.

"Yeah," Tony said.

"I need you to come pick us up." Phil gave him the address.

"On my way."

No sooner had Phil ended the call than his phone rang. It was Gus Nasuti.

"Gus," Phil said. "What can I do for you?"

"You need to let Raph know what's going on. He's mad he hasn't heard from you. Any news?"

"We lost Gabe in the park by Lincoln Drive. We're at the entrance on Germantown. Tony's coming to get us."

"Why is Tony coming for you?"

"Our car was gone when we got back."

"What? Was it stolen?" Gus asked excitedly. "How could anyone steal that car? Doesn't it have a security system?"

"Yeah. I guess it's not fool-proof."

"Wait." Gus chuckled. "Don't tell me Gabe stole your car while you were chasing him in the park."

"Afraid so. They're hard to steal, but apparently Gabe found a way," Phil said. "So you see my predicament."

"You're damn right I do. Look, there's going to be some major backlash. I suggest you let me handle this with the boss. If you bring him the news, he'll explode and you'll be in the line of fire. If I tell him, he'll still explode, but maybe I can calm him down a little before you get here."

"I guess you've got a point," Phil said. "Let me know how it goes."

◆ ◆ ◆

Gus walked up the well-groomed walkway to the D'Angelo home. The daffodils presented a cheerful approach to the house, but Gus knew this was the calm before the storm. On the way in, he noticed the black Denali parked across the street and figured it had been found.

Raph opened the door quickly after Gus rang the doorbell.

"Raph," Gus said, with the utmost politeness. "Mind if I come in?"

"Not at all, my friend," Raph said. "I hope you've got better news than I've been getting."

"Phil and Denny chased Gabe into the park. They almost got him but he was too fast."

"You mean Wissahickon Valley?"

"Yeah. Near Germantown."

"Gabe and I used to go running on those trails when we were younger. He did it a lot more than me and he knows his way around in there. I'm not too surprised he was able to lose those guys."

"Apparently they ran into the park looking for him, but he somehow doubled back to where they left their car and he drove off with it," Gus said in a quiet voice.

"So, Gabe stole their car right out from under them?"

Gus shrugged his shoulders.

Raph took a deep breath and shook his head. "I told those morons Gabe was making fools out of us, and now he's taken it to a whole new level. So, are we going to get our car back? That's what, a seventy, eighty-thousand-dollar car?"

"I think it's already back. Come with me," Gus said, pointing to the front door. When they walked outside, Gus pointed to the large black SUV across the street. "I think that's it," he said.

"Wait a minute, I can't believe this," Raph said as he stormed across the street to the Denali. Gus followed close behind. In a moment the two stood by the front passenger window. Raph cupped his hands around his eyes to look in the tinted windows. "It's Phil's. There's a pack of Marlboro's in the cup holder where he always keeps them." Then he saw the note on the driver's seat. The door was unlocked, so Raph opened it and reached across for the piece of paper. After he read it, he curled it up and threw it on the ground, shaking his head.

"So he was right in front of my house, delivering Phil's car with a note inside. I can't deny the guy's got balls. I wish our guys were half as clever as Gabe. No wonder my father relied on him so much." Raph turned and walked back toward the house.

Gus was surprised at the mild reaction, but he figured it wasn't over yet. When they got inside, it turned out he was correct in his assessment. They entered Raph's office where Raph poured a glass of bourbon and swallowed it in one gulp. Then he poured another one and did the same.

"I know you're gonna tell me that Gabe protected my sister," Raph said, starting to slur his words. "I know because my father asked him to. Why didn't he ask me? He always relied on Gabe. I was the boss's son, but everything was 'Gabe do this,' or 'Gabe do that.' You'd think Michael D'Angelo didn't have a son." Raph threw his glass against the fireplace and sat at his desk.

Gus could hardly believe what he was hearing. "So it's not because Gabe testified, but because your father relied on him more than you?" As consigliere, Gus felt he could ask such a personal question, but only in private.

"You're damn right I'm mad about it. Either way, Gabe needs to go," Raph said, pounding his hand on the desk.

"Did you ever consider that maybe your father was protecting you? You were next in line to run this family. And look at you now, you're the boss. If he had sent you to protect Maria, you might be dead. Gabe was lucky to survive."

"Maybe … maybe, but it goes way beyond that." Raph picked up another glass and filled it. "I may be the boss, but I feel like I've got a bunch of clowns working for me. Phil's my right-hand man, and look at his screw-ups just this week."

"I hear you. But I don't know anyone who could have done better tracking him. And how often does Phil have to deal with someone like Gabe? Gabe operates on a different level than most people."

"So what are you saying? I should hire Gabe back?" Raph asked with a cynical laugh.

"No. Phil is still one of your best men and no one can question his loyalty. But sometimes I wonder if maybe you should consider promoting some new blood into your inner circle."

"I don't know who that would be, but we do need some new talent. I want Phil off the case. We're getting nowhere fast, and he needs to learn that he can't go on letting Gabe get away without consequences."

"Who should we put in charge?"

"I want you in charge. And I want to stay closely involved. We'll need more help too," Raph said.

"How about Rudy Lazarro?" Gus suggested. "He could help with this."

"The Maestro? Not a bad idea. He's a good man and he gets things done. So to repeat: Tell Phil to stand down for now, and you, me, and Maestro will continue to look for Gabe," Raph said, then drained the last of his bourbon.

Chapter 37

The morning after Maria visited Brian in the emergency room, she felt like her stomach was tied in knots. The fact that he asked for "space" was starting to sink in. Was he breaking up with her? A few weeks ago, it seemed like she and Brian were on the verge of getting engaged. Her feelings for Brian did not have the fireworks she had felt when she thought about Gabe, and she had to admit that when Gabe reappeared a few weeks ago, she felt some of the thrill she had experienced when she first met him. But Maria had suppressed those feelings. She was with Brian now, and the path of her life was becoming clear, or so she thought. She had spent a lot of time with Brian and her affection for him had blossomed . He was a good man, and he would make a good father. She didn't want to lose him and she was not going to give up on him.

Maria called the hospital and learned Brian had not been discharged. It was a Saturday morning, so she jumped in her car and drove to the hospital. After clearing hospital security and getting her visitor badge, she hurried to the elevator and walked to his room. The door was half open, and she began to feel nervous. Before she got up her nerve to enter, a man who looked to be about Brian's age walked out of the room. When she looked closer, she realized he was

Brian's brother, Mike. They had met at Thanksgiving dinner a few months ago at Brian's mother's home in Reading.

"Hello, Maria," Mike said.

"Hi Mike. How is Brian doing?"

"The doctor is with him right now, so I'm going to get a cup of coffee in the cafeteria. Do you want anything?"

"Thanks, but I'm good. Are they going to release him today?"

"I guess it depends on what the doctor says."

Maria didn't detect any hostility or negative feelings from Mike. She figured Brian must not have told him the whole story. "I'd like to speak to him after the doctor is finished if you don't mind," she said.

"Go right ahead. I'll be a few minutes anyway."

"Thanks." Maria started pacing up and down the hallway as she waited for the doctor to finish.

◆ ◆ ◆

About two minutes later, the doctor left Brian's room carrying a clipboard and making some notes. Maria didn't like the look on his face. As she entered the room, the look on Brian's face wasn't much better. She spoke first. "Brian, I'm sorry to bother you. I just didn't want to leave things the way we left them yesterday."

Brian didn't say anything. He just looked at Maria with a pained look on his face, so she continued. "I'm so, so sorry for what happened to you. I couldn't sleep at all last night and I missed being here with you. I love you and I want you to get better soon. I know you talked about space. I'll honor that and hope we can spend time together soon."

Brian seemed to nod, but looked straight ahead, deep in thought. "They're not letting me go home today."

"What's wrong? Is everything okay?"

"The doctor came in to discuss my CT scan. There's no concussion or bleeding in my brain."

"That's good news, right?"

"He said the scan shows something on the front lobe of my brain that he didn't like. It has nothing to do with my injuries."

"Did he say what it was?" she asked.

"All he said was it was concerning, and they are going to hook me up with a neurologist. He's coming around later today to see me."

"I'm sure everything will be okay. I'll stay if you like. Or if there's anything you'd like me to bring you, I can do that too."

"No, that's not necessary. I have a headache and I'd like to rest a while," he said. "Maybe this thing they found explains all the headaches I've been getting."

"I didn't realize you were having headaches." Maria sighed and shook her head. "Oh Brian, I hope everything is okay. Can I call you in a day or two to see how you are?"

"Sure," he said and closed his eyes.

"Okay, I'll leave you to rest," she said as she put her hand on his.

CHAPTER 38

Gabe found a small motel just outside Barto, Pennsylvania. It was a small town about fifty miles northwest of Philadelphia nestled among farms and rolling hills. Other than a few gas stations and a grocery store, there wasn't much in the town, just a Catholic shrine people came to visit. Gabe was sure no one had seen him traveling, and he was certain the D'Angelo family would never think of looking for him there. Still, he had to be careful. He decided not to tell Maria his precise location so she could deny knowing where he was if anyone asked.

The Pleasant Motel, off Route 100, was where he crashed after leaving the city. It was small and inexpensive, but clean. The proprietor was a woman in her fifties named Shirley, and she lived in an apartment behind the office. She came across as flirtatious, so Gabe played along and struck up a friendly conversation with her. While he paid in cash and checked in under one of the false identities he maintained, Shirley made sure he was aware that her husband had died. Gabe concluded she wasn't really making a play for him, she was just lonely and happy to have a handsome young man to talk to.

The next morning, Gabe got up and had a cup of coffee from the pot in the office Shirley maintained for guests next to a stand full of brochures on tourist attractions. He felt comfortable with the situation and paid for another night.

Shirley seemed genuinely happy that he wasn't leaving. "I'm glad to have you stay another night. I don't get many repeat customers," she said with a smirk.

"Where do your customers come from?" Gabe asked. He figured the more he knew about the clientele the better, for his safety and security.

"We get a lot of pilgrims coming to the shrine. They come from all over. A lot of nuns and clergy. Otherwise, it's mostly people just passing through like yourself."

"I'm not exactly passing through. My wife filed for divorce, and her lawyer is trying to take me to the cleaners. I just needed to lay low for a few days. They want to serve me with some subpoenas." Maybe it was Maria's influence on him, but Gabe was getting tired of this life where he had to tell so many lies. But the story was harmless and gave him cover.

"Are there any children involved?" Shirley asked as she wiped off the countertop with a dust rag.

"Fortunately, no. She cheated on me and now she wants to leave and take most of our assets, even though I helped her pay for law school. So go figure."

"You poor thing," she said.

Gabe figured he had her on his side. "I hope if anyone comes looking for me, you'll help me out."

"Absolutely. If there's anything else I can do for you, please let me know. You seem like a good man. My brother had a similar situation a few years ago and he got burned bad in his divorce, even though he didn't deserve it."

"Thanks so much," Gabe said.

"Do you work anywhere nearby?" she asked.

"No, I can work remotely as long as I can get a Wi-Fi connection."

"We have Wi-Fi. Did you have any trouble connecting?'

"No, everything is fine," Gabe said. He remembered that he was expecting an email from Maria, but he'd need to retrieve it from a public computer where he would put the video on a flash drive. In the meantime, he could leave the video on the server until he needed it.

"There's also a coffee shop about two miles down the road. It's not like Starbucks. It's an independent shop with a cozy atmosphere. They have great muffins and they offer free Wi-Fi. The owner is a friend of mine."

Gabe took note but didn't want to get too involved. The last thing he needed was for the two business owners to be trading stories about a nice young man passing through town. Such stories had a way of spreading. When he left the office, he went back to his room and checked the news on his laptop. He was pleased to see the news about the murder in Warminster had died down. After searching, all he could find were statements from local police that the crime remained under investigation. He decided to look up the shrine that Shirley had mentioned. He felt it was time for a visit and a risk worth taking.

◆　◆　◆

After stopping for a coffee and muffin at the shop Shirley had recommended, Gabe drove to the shrine. It was dedicated to Padre Pio, an Italian priest who ministered during the early twentieth century, mostly in a small town in Italy. He was a mystic known for his humility and devotion who, during a period of his life, showed stigmata on his hands resembling the wounds of Christ.

Gabe found a large well-kept property with manicured gardens and a long portico leading to a series of modern, tan buildings that might or might not have been a church. Gabe walked toward the portico, which covered a pathway to the largest building with a reddish orange tiled roof. It reminded him of pictures of Italy. Inside, he found a museum and gift shop and a hallway leading to a large chapel with a vaulted ceiling. Unlike other Catholic Churches he had visited, this one was bright and airy. Religious paintings and statues graced the wall and sides of the sanctuary.

Gabe sat in a pew about midway to the front and closed his eyes for a few moments. Although there were a few pilgrims in the chapel, it was quiet and comfortable. Gabe had not spent much time in church, but he felt a sense of peace as he sat taking in the surroundings. Up front on the left side was a booth where he assumed priests heard confessions. He began to think how great it would be if he could simply unload all his burdens and turn from the lifestyle he had led for so many years, but it didn't seem possible—at least not yet.

Gabe began to think of the life before him and what it held if he didn't break free of his dangerous entanglement with the D'Angelo family. And he had abandoned the witness protection program and had not reported to his parole officer as required by his sentence. Gabe knew there was a warrant out for his arrest, but he felt that with the evidence he had compiled against his former associates, as well as the video Maria had of Phil Morino, he had a fighting chance to make a deal to get back on track with his parole. He might need to go to prison for a while as a slap on the wrist, but serving some time seemed doable. Gabe was more worried about the punishment the D'Angelo family could inflict on him in prison than the thought of prison itself—at least as long as Raphael D'Angelo was in charge of the family. Finally, at the back of his mind was the fantasy he clung to about Maria. No matter what he was able to achieve or how he might get out of his predicament, it seemed empty without her in the picture.

Gabe sat back in the pew and closed his eyes. Before he realized it, he was whispering a prayer, asking for God's help to see the right path forward. He had been raised in the church as a child, but he hadn't attended a mass in many years. The sense of peace he had felt when he first sat down in the pew became greater, almost overwhelming him. He sat for a while longer, and ideas began to form. He realized the shrine could be a good place for him to stay under the radar. And with Maria's background, no one would think anything about Maria coming here to deliver the video (if she couldn't email it) or even just to visit if he could persuade her to do so. She'd be hesitant about coming just to visit due to her existing relationship; if only she weren't committed to Brian, Gabe thought.

Gabe was so engrossed in his thoughts he didn't see the priest in the back of the chapel squinting to see him better. The priest wore a long black robe that extended all the way to the floor with a row of buttons from his neck all the way to his feet. He quietly walked around to the side of the chapel to get a better look. When he was about a row behind Gabe in the side aisle, he paused. The priest knew photos were not permitted in the sanctuary, so he slid into the pew and knelt, as if to pray. He pulled out an iPhone and hit the camera icon, holding the phone just below the back of the pew in front of him. When Gabe's head turned slightly to the right, the priest quickly snapped a picture of his profile. The priest devoutly crossed himself and silently tiptoed to the narthex and out the large doors.

◆　◆　◆

The priest walked briskly through the portico toward the lot where his car was parked and got in. He immediately dialed the number he had for Raphael D'Angelo.

Raph didn't recognize the caller, but was curious who it was since he rarely gave out his phone number, so he answered.

"Who is this?"

"Mr. D'Angelo, this is Father Pierce."

Raph immediately recognized the name and voice since Father Pierce had visited his mother in the hospital and conducted her funeral.

"Yes, Father Pierce. What can I do for you?" Raph had paid the priest a handsome honorarium for the mass and was curious why he would be calling. Raph rarely attended church.

"It's been a week since the funeral. I wanted to check in and see how you and your family were doing. I know how hard it is to lose a parent."

"We're fine, Father. My mother was a very devout woman as you know, and she lived a full life. One of the most important things she taught us was to pick up and move on when we face difficulties, so that's what I'm trying to do," Raph said, feeling proud that he had made up such a good answer on the spot. In reality, he hadn't learned much from his mother.

"I'm glad to hear you are doing as well as can be expected," said Father Pierce. "Oh, one more thing. I'm on the board of the Padre Pio Foundation, which supports a shrine in Barto, a little past Pottstown. I was there for a board meeting this weekend and stayed over."

Raph thought this was leading up to a pitch for a donation to the shrine, so he was not expecting what Father Pierce said next.

"There was a young man I met a few years ago. A Mr. Rossi. He was getting a little too friendly with your sister when she was living at the convent as I recall, which caused some concerns. Then, if my memory serves me, he played a role in your father's trial."

"Yes, what about him?"

"Well, I'm pretty sure I saw him today in the chapel at the Padre Pio shrine. I don't really know him so I didn't speak to him, but I heard that the police were looking for him and I thought you might want to know. I'm forwarding a picture I took."

"Thanks for letting me know." Raph clicked on the priest's text. Yeah, that's him. Did you happen to see where he went after leaving the church?"

"No. I left before he did. He could still be sitting in the chapel for all I know."

"Well, thank you for calling, but I need to be somewhere and I'm running late. Thanks again," Raph said as he disconnected the call and immediately dialed Gus Nasuti.

"Raph. What's up?"

"I just got a lead on Gabe. I spoke to my mother's priest and he just saw Gabe at some sort of shrine out in Barto. He was there when the priest left and still might be there."

"Where the hell is Barto?"

"Somewhere out near Pottstown. I think it's less than an hour away. We need to get out there. How fast can you and Maestro get here?"

"We can be there in less than half an hour. We're on our way."

"Wait. We'll waste half an hour if we meet here first. Go right to the shrine. Look it up. There can't be more than one Catholic shrine in Barto. I'll see you there. Let me know when you get there and I'll do the same," Raph said excitedly. *Sooner or later, Gabe's luck will run out. Maybe this is the day.*

CHAPTER 39

It was Sunday morning. Maria had gone to early Mass at her church and spent considerable time praying for Brian's healing and recovery. She also prayed he would somehow forgive her—she knew that her actions had led to the home invasion and the terrible beating he had suffered. As soon as she left the church, she called the hospital and discovered he was still there. Within fifteen minutes, she was entering the parking garage for the hospital. Since it was a Sunday, she had no trouble finding a spot.

When she entered Brian's room, the staff was picking up his breakfast dishes. Brian was dressed in his street clothes and was stretched out on the bed.

"Brian. How are you?" Maria noticed the bruises on his face were looking better. "It looks like they're letting you go home."

"Thanks for coming, Maria," Brian said, much to Maria's surprise. "I'm not going home yet. I need surgery."

"Really? Because of the problem on the CT scan?"

"Yes. The neurologist was here yesterday and said he was concerned," Brian said as he began to break down. "He said it looked like a glioblastoma."

"A what?"

"If the neurologist turns out to be right, it's a brain tumor and it's cancerous."

"Oh my gosh!" Maria said, wrinkling her brow. "You'll be okay after they remove it, won't you?"

"It's very serious."

"Yes, but I'm sure there are good surgeons here that can remove it and then you'll be fine, right?" Maria drew closer to Brian's bed.

"I don't know. They can't do it here. They're taking me to Jefferson Hospital in Philadelphia. Apparently they have a top-notch surgeon there. They're going to admit me today and do the surgery tomorrow or the day after if all goes as planned."

"Oh my gosh!" Maria said again, placing her hand over her heart. "That's so soon!"

"Yeah, they said it's important to do it as soon as possible."

"So, it sounds like they caught it early. That's always good."

"I'm sorry again for the things I said, and I am really glad you're here."

"There's nothing to be sorry for," Maria said. "You had a very painful, scary experience. I'm the one who should be sorry."

"Don't be. If I hadn't been attacked last week, I wouldn't have had the CT scan and my condition wouldn't have been discovered until my symptoms got worse, and it would have been much harder to treat. God moves in mysterious ways."

"Yes, that's true. But I still wish you hadn't gone through that. Now, I know you're going to need help. How are you getting to Jefferson?"

"Mike is going to drive me. He'll be here soon, and we're supposed to leave before noon. They offered to take me down in an ambulance, but I turned it down."

"Can I visit you tonight at Jefferson?" Maria asked.

"It's a long drive and it's hard to park. Plus, they are going to have me in and out of the room for tests. How about if we just do FaceTime when I'm back in my room?"

"I really don't mind making the trip, but Facetime is fine if you think that's better."

"Maybe tomorrow after the surgery. But I don't know when I'm going to be done. I'll call you when I'm able to have visitors."

Just then, Brian's brother walked in. "Is the patient ready? Oh, hi Maria," Mike said, turning to her with a smile.

"Hi Mike. I would have been happy to drive Brian down to Jefferson."

"No problem. I've been staying at his place and I got a bag packed for him, not that he needs a lot of clothes for this trip."

"Brian, I'll call or Facetime tonight, and hopefully tomorrow I can come down and see you," she said, looking right at Brian.

"Thanks, Maria. I hope we can connect," Brian said.

"We better get going. I'm in front of the hospital in the pickup zone, so I can't leave my car there long," Mike said as he helped Brian into a wheelchair.

Maria leaned over and gave Brian a kiss, this time on the lips. "I'll talk to you soon," she said as Mike wheeled Brian into the hallway and down to the elevator.

◆　◆　◆

As soon as Maria got home, she went to her computer and looked up "glioblastoma;" she was shocked by what she read. It was an aggressive brain tumor with a heartbreaking prognosis—few people with the disease live beyond two years. Brian's young age and good health were factors that might help him live longer, but it was an incurable and terminal. "No, this can't be!" she screamed as she read the words on the screen. Her chest tightened and she began to breathe rapidly.

Brian had already suffered a brutal beating. Now he would experience more suffering, both from the treatment for his cancer and the symptoms of the disease itself, which would surely tighten their grip on him in the coming months. The fact that there was nothing she could do made it worse. Brian was a good, kind man and he didn't deserve this. Maria had felt grief when her mother died, but it was nothing like this. Her mother had lived a full life, and her passing was a relief from the disease that afflicted her more and more each day. Brian had nearly his whole life before him, and Maria wanted to be a part of it. Now she had no one except God to talk to; she spent much of the afternoon pouring her heart out in prayer. Maria had lost track of time when her phone rang. It was Rose.

"Rose?" Maria said when she picked up. "Is everything okay?"

"I don't know. I'm having a really hard time. Raph hasn't been himself. I hardly see him. He used to be so nice and considerate. Now, he doesn't even talk to me and he hardly pays attention to Tessa. Some nights he doesn't come home, and when he's here, he's cooped up in that office of his with the door closed." Rose coughed and cleared her throat. "Just now I heard him take a phone call and right afterward he ran out. I asked him where he was going and he just said 'out' and slammed the door."

"I'm sorry," Maria said. "Do you have any idea what's going on?" She had a good idea, but wanted to see if there was something else.

"I don't know. I guess it's the nature of the business he's in," Rose said with a sigh.

"I should have called to check on you, but I've had some trials of my own."

"Really, what's wrong?"

"It's Brian," she said. "He had a break-in at his house and the intruders beat him up."

"That's terrible! Is he okay?

"Actually no. I mean, he'll be okay from the break-in, but they gave him a CT scan at the hospital and he's got a tumor on his brain. He's having surgery down at Jefferson either tomorrow or the next day."

"That poor man. Brian is so nice. I can't bear to think of him with a serious illness," Rose said. "He always seems so happy just to be with you."

"I know. I'm really worried." Maria paused a moment as she wiped a tear that ran down her face. "What about you. Is there anything I can do to help?"

"Maybe we can console each other. Do you want to come over tonight? I was going to order a pizza for Tess and me. If the past is any guide, Raph won't be back until late, if at all."

"Okay," Maria said reluctantly. She wanted to help Rose but didn't want to get into a discussion about Raph's ongoing pursuit of Gabe. And she certainly didn't want to tell her that Raph's right-hand man had threatened her.

"Great! Tessa will be thrilled you're coming."

"I can't stay long. I need to call Brian tonight and I have a big day tomorrow. I need to be at school early, and I'll probably go downtown to visit Brian afterward," Maria said.

"That's no problem. Can you come around six?" Rose asked.

"Sure thing."

CHAPTER 40

Gabe had not planned on staying for the mass that took place after he had sat in the chapel pew, but he was glad he did. It brought back happy memories of his childhood when his mother took him to church. It also gave him satisfaction to imagine what Maria would think of his coming back to church. She would surely approve. He had already spent more than two hours at the shrine and figured it was time to leave. He got up, left though the narthex, and walked down a corridor to a set of glass doors. He saw a large black SUV enter the parking lot and pull into a spot, and when the passenger door opened, Gus Nasuti emerged. The driver got out and Gabe squinted. It was Rudy Lazarro, the Maestro. It was unusual to see Gus in the field, but Raph no doubt had ordered all hands on deck to find him. Gabe's car was on the other side of the parking lot, which meant he would have to walk in plain view of Gus and Rudy to reach it.

Gabe did some quick thinking as he watched Gus and the Maestro survey the scene. He figured they would probably walk right to the doors where he stood. Recalling another set of doors on the other side of the complex where he could exit while his pursuers were checking out the interior, he began walking quickly in that direction. He slipped out the doors and cautiously looked around in case Gus or Rudy had gone around to cover the back while the other came in the front. Neither of them was in sight as Gabe slipped out. When he looked back in, he saw Gus and Rudy enter and walk up to an information desk. It was hard to see, but it looked like Rudy was showing a picture to the lady at the desk. Hopefully she hadn't noticed Gabe walking down the corridor. She shook her head no and pointed in the direction of the chapel.

How in the world did they find me here?

◆　◆　◆

"We just got here," Gus said to Raph on his cell phone. "It's big, so it'll take a little time to search the place."

"I'm less than two minutes out. We need to cover the exits to make sure he doesn't slip out."

"When you get here, why don't you hang near the front doors by the parking lot. If there's another door around back, I'll have Rudy hang there."

As Raph pulled into the parking lot, he slowed down and scoped out the area with a small pair of binoculars. He called Gus. "I got eyes on him!" Raph shouted. "He's in the parking lot getting in a car. It's a small, dark gray sedan." Raph felt for his pistol in a shoulder holster under his windbreaker. By the time Raph got closer, Gabe had pulled way toward the parking lot exit that led to a long, two-lane access road and the highway. "I'm gonna follow him. Let's stay connected and I'll let you know which direction we're going."

Raph sped through the parking lot. An older couple gave him a dirty look for going so fast, but Raph was undeterred. Gabe had reached the end of the access road and was waiting to pull out onto the highway. As Raph got closer, Gabe turned left onto the highway, accelerating much faster than normal. Raph wondered if he'd been made.

"He just turned left onto the highway and he's moving fast," Raph said.

"Just keep him in view and we'll catch up," Gus said as he and Rudy walked quickly toward the front entrance.

◆ ◆ ◆

As Gabe waited at the end of the access road for an opening in the traffic to pull onto the highway, he looked in the rearview mirror and saw a black Mercedes S500 zooming toward him. He knew it was Raph; he also knew his little Honda could not outrun the V-8 engine in Raph's Mercedes, and that Gus and the Maestro would be along shortly. Gabe had studied the local roads between the shrine and his motel to be prepared for situations like this and knew his evasive driving skills were far better than Raph's ability behind the wheel. He turned left and headed south, where he knew he could take advantage of several small towns with side streets and turn-offs. Luckily, he was able to pull out in front of a large, slow-moving delivery truck. With oncoming traffic, Raph would not be able to pass the truck, and his view of Gabe's car would be obstructed. Gabe knew he had only a few minutes before Gus and Rudy caught up, and Rudy was driving an SUV with a V8 engine that would be as fast as Raph's Mercedes. Then, Gabe saw his chance.

Up ahead was a traffic light where the small road crossed a highway. The light was green, but Gabe slowed his car down, slowing all the traffic behind him. The light turned yellow, and Gabe decelerated even more, causing the delivery truck driver behind him to honk his horn angrily. The light turned red just as he approached the intersection, and Gabe stopped. After looking for cars coming from the left, he made a right turn onto the highway heading south. In his rearview mirror, he could see the truck inch forward, but it remained at the light. Gabe assumed Raph saw him make his right turn, but he still had a chance to put some distance between him and his pursuers, even if only for a minute or so.

Gabe floored it, hoping there were no police in the area. As soon as he went around a slight bend where he couldn't be seen, he turned left onto a small side road. When the light turned green and Raph was able to turn right , he wouldn't know whether Gabe turned off the highway or not, or if he turned right or left down one of the many side roads. Gabe continued driving on the back roads, making a few turns, until he came to Highway 73, where he turned left and headed east. Gabe noticed that he had just taken a shortcut, cutting off the corner to get to this highway. If Raph and his crew continued in the direction Gabe had gone at the intersection, they might guess he had taken Highway 73 and they would turn east on it too, so he wasn't out of danger yet. Gabe looked at Google Maps as he drove. He discovered he could drive some back roads east to Route 309, one of the older highways that ran toward the Philadelphia suburbs on the north side. Since a quick check in his rearview mirror confirmed no one was following him, he decided it was time to get back to the city.

◆　◆　◆

Raph pounded his hand on the dashboard as he sat behind the delivery truck at the traffic light. There was no room on the right side to go around the truck, and there was a steady flow of oncoming traffic on the left side, mostly vehicles on Route 100 that had turned onto the road. He picked up his phone.

"Are you guys on the way?"

"Yeah, there were a bunch of cars leaving the shrine, so we had to wait in line to get out on the road. Do you have eyes on Gabe?" Gus asked.

"I'm at the traffic light about a mile down the road, sitting behind a delivery truck. Gabe got ahead of the truck and slowed us down, so we got hit with a red light. He turned right at the light."

"So he got away?"

"I can't see him right now," Raph said.

Just then, the light turned green, and the delivery truck began to accelerate slowly. After what seemed like half a minute, Raph entered the intersection and turned right.

"Okay, I'm on the road he took, but I still don't see him." Raph shook his head and cursed to himself. "So what do you suggest I do now?"

"Keep driving on that road. We'll catch up to you in a minute or two."

Raph continued driving but there was no sign of Gabe. "You still there?" he asked into his phone.

"Yeah. Any luck?"

"No. I'm starting to pass side roads. He could have turned off on any of them."

"Okay, why don't you find a place to pull over. We'll be there in a minute and we can try and figure this out. I'll have Rudy look at the map for anything that might give us a clue to where he went."

In less than two minutes, Gus and Rudy pulled up behind Raph in the gravel along the side of the road. Gus walked up and knocked on Raph's window. "There's no way we can tell where he went just by looking at the map. But what if he's headed back to hook up with your sister? After all, she's been helping him up to now."

"I guess that's as good a guess as any. So we take the most direct route to Maple Grove?"

"That's what I was thinking. Rudy says we need to get to Route 309, and that will take us there. We'll keep our eyes open."

CHAPTER 41

Gabe got to Route 309 in less than forty-five minutes and began heading south toward Philadelphia. As he drove, he wondered whether on some level he took that route so that he would travel through Maple Grove, where Maria lived and worked. He had to admit he probably did choose the route for that reason and realized Raph and his henchmen would probably make the same assumption. Since he wasn't in a hurry to get anywhere, he decided to test his thinking and see if he was being followed. He found a McDonald's near a corner with a traffic light where he could park inconspicuously and observe the cars driving through the intersection. Even if they didn't have to stop for the light, most cars would slow down. When Gabe was positioned, he pulled the small pair of binoculars out of his bag. It didn't take long to find the answer he sought.

Gabe saw a black Mercedes heading east. As it approached the light, the driver appeared to be Raph. Another large, black SUV followed immediately behind, and he could make out the dark shadows of Gus and Rudy through the tinted window. The two cars slowed as they passed through the intersection, and Gabe decided to follow them—the last thing they would expect him to do. He started his car and pulled out into traffic, just making it through the intersection as the light turned yellow. He stayed back a few cars as he couldn't afford to be detected—he was outnumbered and outgunned, and his little car wouldn't be a match for the D'Angelo vehicles. As they approached Montgomeryville, the traffic picked up a little, and Gabe had to work hard to keep the caravan of his pursuers in view while still staying out of their line of sight.

There was a major junction of highways coming up in Fort Washington, about fifteen minutes down the road. Gabe figured one or both of the SUVs would turn off in another direction there if not before. Gabe's prediction came true sooner than he expected; he saw Raph make a right turn—leaving Gus and Rudy to proceed further—probably heading toward the expressway into the city. Gabe knew the area well since he had visited Maria in the convent, which was just a few minutes away. Gabe made the turn to follow Raph. When they got to Chestnut Hill, it was clear Raph was heading home. Gabe decided to back off and found an inconspicuous place to park just off Germantown Avenue. He picked up his phone and called Maria.

"Hello," she said.

"How is everything?" he asked.

"Not good. Brian is at Jefferson Hospital in the city and he's got a tumor on his brain," she replied with a slight tremor in her voice.

"He didn't get it from being attacked, did he?"

"No. It was already there. But he needed a CT scan because of his injuries, which is how they discovered it."

"I'm so sorry, Maria. That's so sad."

"I'm supposed to have dinner with Rose and Tessa tonight since Raph is out, but I'm worried about Brian and don't really feel like going anywhere. I think I'm going to call and cancel."

"I hope he's going to be okay. How are they going to treat him?"

"I just spoke to him, and they're sending him for an MRI first thing in the morning. Then he'll have surgery to remove the tumor either tomorrow or the next day. So where are you and are you okay?" she asked.

"I'm fine. I stayed outside the city, but I think it's best you don't know where I am right now."

"I understand. Do you have a place to stay?"

"I'm working on it," Gabe said.

"Just so you know, I emailed the video of Phil Morino to the address you gave me," she said.

"Great."

◆　◆　◆

Gabe got a thrill out of following someone who wanted to kill him, but he had had enough of Raph D'Angelo for one day. He picked up his cell phone.

"Hello, Lucy?" he said when the person he called picked up.

"Yes, who is this?"

"It's Gabe. I met you at the tavern on Germantown Avenue about a week ago."

"Oh yes! I'm glad you called."

"Listen, you invited me to your place and I was wondering if I could come by for a visit. I'll explain why when I get there."

"Sure, that would be fine. Give me about a half hour to clean up."

"No problem."

"Why don't you come for dinner?"

"That would really be great. So, I'll see you in about a half hour?"

"I'll be here."

Gabe hung up and saw a small liquor store on the corner not far from his car. It was taking a risk, but he decided to do it anyway. He put on his sunglasses, pulled his baseball cap down in the front, and trotted up to the shop. He bought a bottle of Kendall Jackson Chardonnay, which was a favorite of his. He hoped Lucy would like it as well. Even though her apartment was only a few blocks away, he decided to drive and see if he could get a parking spot closer to the entrance to her building. He got a spot about half a block from the door and sat in the car listening to the radio to make sure he didn't arrive too early. After thirty minutes had passed since they spoke, Gabe walked up to the entrance. He rang Lucy's bell and she buzzed him in. When he arrived at her apartment, Lucy opened the door.

"I'm sorry for inviting myself over to your home on such short notice. Here's a little something to make up for it," Gabe said, handing her the bottle of wine. Gabe noticed she was wearing makeup and perfume.

"Thank you," she said. "And it's no problem. I didn't have any plans for the evening. Come in and have a seat. You said you had something to explain?" Lucy asked, raising her eyebrows.

Gabe had decided to go with the story about being divorced, like he had used at the motel. "I didn't tell you when I saw you before, but I'm in the middle of a divorce. I worked to help put my wife through law school, and now her lawyer is trying to take me to the cleaners. She wants the house and half of our small savings account. She's even asking for alimony, even though she's on track to earn way more than I do."

"Oh, I'm sorry to hear that. My ex did the same thing to me. But why did you need to explain it to me?"

"Her lawyer is trying to subpoena all my records, so I need to lay low while I get some things in order," he explained, not knowing if it was realistic or not, but it sounded plausible.

"I assume you're looking for a place to stay where they can't find you."

"At least for a few days."

"I'm heating up some lasagna and I need to take it out of the oven. Can you excuse me for a moment?"

"That sounds great," Gabe said, noting she didn't respond to his need for a place to stay. He wondered if he had offended her by being so forward. He would see how things went during dinner.

Lucy returned with two glasses of wine. She sat on the couch next to him. "The lasagna needs to cool off a little," she said.

Gabe took a sip. Of course it was the Kendall Jackson he had brought. "Was the fitness center open today?"

"Not on Sundays. I used to keep it open, but not many people came, and I didn't want to hang around there without much to do."

"So you decide when it's open?"

"Yes, I'm the owner. Are you into fitness?"

"I used to be, big time. Now it's harder to find the time to go to the gym on a regular basis."

"You said you were away for a while?"

"I was in the Saint Louis area working, but I missed Philadelphia. It's where I grew up."

Lucy took a sip of the chardonnay. "This is good. What was the name of it?" she asked.

"Kendall Jackson. It's from California."

"So, Gabe. What are your plans? I mean when you get through the divorce proceedings."

"I'd like to stay in the area if I can."

"Was your wife with you in St. Louis?"

"No, she's around here. We've been separated for a year. At first we thought some time apart would help us come together again, but it didn't work out. Liz is about to graduate from law school and she's starting at a firm this summer. She's got new friends and new interests, and I don't really fit into her plans."

"That's too bad. Where did she go to law school?" Lucy asked.

"Villanova."

Lucy got up to serve the dinner. Gabe knew the conversation was dragging, and he didn't feel the electricity he had felt when he met Lucy at the bar. At least she wasn't asking difficult or probing questions. And even though it was not turning out to be an exciting evening, Gabe perceived that Lucy was lonely and was glad to have the company, which surprised him since she was an attractive woman. She beckoned him to a small dining table in the next room by the kitchen.

"This looks great," Gabe said as he looked at the small tray of lasagna, bowls of salad, and dinner rolls.

Lucy smiled, appreciating the compliment, and started dishing out the meal. "So, what about other family in the area?" she asked.

"Not much at all," Gabe said. "My dad died when I was six, and my mother died four years ago. I had a brother who got into trouble and died of a drug overdose. Liz has family, and I had a great relationship with them, but when our marriage started to go south, they all seemed to turn against me."

"I'm so sorry to hear that. Both of my parents are alive and they live down at the Jersey Shore. I spend weekends in the summer there if I can get someone to cover the business on Saturdays. I'm divorced. My husband was in the army and we moved around a lot. Then he got deployed overseas and things went downhill. When he came home on leave, he wasn't the same. I wondered whether he was having an affair when he was away, but I couldn't get him to talk to me. When he developed a temper and started verbally abusing me, I said enough is enough. We've been divorced for three years."

After a while, Lucy got up and started carrying dishes to the kitchen.

"Let me help you," Gabe said as Lucy came beside him to get his plate.

"No. You just sit right there," she said, putting a soft hand on his shoulder. Gabe began to feel the electricity again. She came back in a moment and refilled his wine glass.

"Are you up for dessert?" she asked.

"No, I'm good." Gabe wondered if he should bring up the subject of a place to stay again, then decided to wait.

"If you change your mind, there's a really good ice cream parlor about two blocks away. We could walk over there."

"Maybe," Gabe said. "I'm feeling a little tired right now." Going for a walk on the main street of Germantown was the last thing he wanted to do. For all he knew, Raph had his soldiers patrolling the streets.

"Okay, let's take our wine glasses back to the sitting room." Lucy carried the tray of leftover lasagna back to the kitchen. "I feel warm, do you?" she asked, unbuttoning the top two buttons of her blouse. "If you need a place to crash for a few nights, you're welcome to stay, as long as we're clear that it's just a few days."

"Understood," Gabe answered.

"I like you, Gabe, and I like having you around so far, but we hardly know each other. So, there's a spare room with a futon. I think that will be the most comfortable for you."

"I can't tell you how much I appreciate this."

CHAPTER 42

Raph slammed the front door and stormed into the house, heading straight for his office.

"What's wrong, Daddy?" Tessa was playing with a dollhouse on the floor of the family room.

"Nothing, Tessa," he replied as he strode by her.

"You don't ever seem to have time for your daughter," Rose said with a sneer as she came into the family room from the kitchen, but Raph had already closed the door. She could hear him shouting in the office. Rose was sorry Maria had called to cancel, but she understood Maria had bigger problems on her mind relating to Brian. She also knew it wasn't a good idea for Maria to come while Raph was on a rampage.

Rose didn't give up easily. "Tessa, honey, could you take your toys up to your bedroom for a few minutes?"

"Are we still getting pizza tonight?" Tessa asked.

"Yes, in a little while. I just need you to go upstairs for now and I'll call you when it's time."

Tessa gathered up her toys and went to the steps.

Rose walked quietly to the door of Raph's office. Raph was talking on the phone in more hushed tones now. "Raph, we need to talk," she said, loud enough to be sure he heard her. There was no response.

She tested the doorknob, and it was locked. "Open the damn door, Raph!" she yelled as she began to pound on the door.

Rose heard footsteps inside the study. Raph opened the door. "Can't you hear? I'm busy on a phone call."

"All I hear is that you're too busy to talk to you wife and daughter. It's Sunday evening, for heaven's sake. Don't you ever have time for your family?"

"I'm sorry but something important came up. I'm in charge of this operation and I need to deal with things no matter what day it is."

"But it's been like this every day. You can't have that much to deal with. Don't you have people working for you?"

"Sometimes being in charge means you have more to do to keep everybody in line."

"This is all about Gabe isn't it? Ever since he came back here you've been obsessed. Can't you just leave that poor man alone? He saved your sister's life."

"That may or may not be true. But you know the rules. You're not supposed to ask me about my work, much less question decisions I make."

"So, I'm right. This is all about Gabe. Well, Raph, if anything happens to Gabe, Maria will never forgive you," she said, almost shouting.

"I wouldn't be much of a leader if I based my decisions on how my sister feels. She has nothing to do with our business. She never has. And why is she so concerned? Doesn't she have a boyfriend?"

"She still cares about Gabe, and her boyfriend is very sick. He's got a brain tumor."

"A brain tumor? We didn't do that to him," Raph said, instantly regretting his choice of words.

"What do you mean you didn't do that to him?"

"Nothing. I'm sorry about her boyfriend and hope he gets well," Raph said as he closed the door and retreated into his office.

Chapter 43

That evening, Maria dialed Jefferson Hospital and asked to be connected to Brian's room to see if there was any news. The phone rang a number of times, but eventually Brian picked up.

"Hi Brian. I'm just calling to see how you're doing," Maria said.

"Sorry, I had trouble getting to the phone. Yeah, I guess I'm okay. I have my MRI scheduled for first thing in the morning, but the way things go around here, who knows when that will be. I've learned that hospitals run on a different time schedule. When they promise something will happen soon, it means whenever they get around to it."

"Sorry you have to wait so long. How are you feeling?"

"I have a little headache and I felt dizzy when I got up earlier. I felt the same way several times in the past few weeks but never gave any thought to it. Now they're telling me it might be a symptom of my condition."

Tears began forming in Maria's eyes. Brian was so young and should be enjoying life. They should be discussing plans to get married and have a family. Instead, Brian was in the hospital waiting for a surgery in which the doctors would open his skull and remove a tumor from his brain. Maria swallowed and took a deep breath. "I'm so sorry you have to be in the hospital right now, but I'm sure the doctors will get you through this," she said with a tremor in her voice.

"Thank you. You're a compassionate and caring person, and I thank God for the time I've been able to spend getting to know you these past few years. You've really brought happiness into my life. I'm sorry for the misunderstandings we've had."

"You have nothing to feel sorry for, and I'm thankful for our time together as well, but you sound like it's coming to an end. It's not. It's just beginning for us. You're young and healthy, and like I said, you'll get through this."

Neither one spoke for a moment, but Maria eventually broke the silence. "What about your surgery? Any update on when they'll do the surgery?" she asked.

"It's probably going to be the day after tomorrow. They need to get me through the MRI and then they need some time to study the results and line up the staff to help. Apparently, there's some careful planning for this procedure and they like to start the surgery early in the day, so they won't be able to do that tomorrow."

"What about your doctor, the one who is going to perform the surgery? Do you know anything about him?"

"It's Dr. Berenson. All I know is that everybody tells me I'm lucky to have him. He's one of the top doctors here. Otherwise, I don't know a lot about him. When he comes in, there's no small talk. It's strictly business."

"I'm glad you've got a good surgeon. It's an answer to my prayers," Maria said.

"I guess so. I just want to get this over with."

"You're a very brave man. I'd be a mess if I were in the hospital waiting for surgery like this. I really admire your calmness and strength."

"Well, it's not as though I have much choice in the matter. I feel like I'm not really in control of my circumstances."

"It's too bad you have to wait around so long for it. Can I swing by tomorrow? Is there anything you need?" Maria was thinking she would surprise Brian with a copy of John Grisham's latest novel. They had been talking about it recently and how it hadn't been available at the library because all the copies were checked out and the waiting list was long.

"That would be great. I'll be tied up in the morning with the test, but why don't you call as soon as school is finished and I can tell you if my schedule is clear."

"Sounds good."

"How is your family drama playing out? Is your brother still on the warpath?"

Maria was surprised Brian could discuss her family so calmly after what had happened to him. "I haven't heard much. I know my brother is still looking for Gabe, but as you suggested, I'm stepping back and not getting involved. I'm sure Gabe can take care of himself. Right now, I'm a little worried about Rose and Tessa. It's not easy for Rose to be married to someone like Raph. I bet sometimes she's wondering what she got herself into."

"I'm sure she went into her marriage with her eyes wide open."

"I was supposed to go over and have dinner with her and Tessa, but I cancelled. It didn't feel right going out to dinner right now ..." Maria said before cutting herself off. She didn't want Brian to know how worried she was about him.

"I'm sorry you had to cancel, but I'm glad you're available to talk. My brother had to drive back to Reading to take care of some things, but he'll be back the day of the surgery. This is kind of a lonely place even though it's a beehive of activity."

"Any idea how long they will keep you after the surgery?" she asked.

"I've been asking the same question and all I get is that they will need to observe me for a few days. So no, I don't really know."

CHAPTER 44

After helping her clean up from dinner, Gabe sat with Lucy and talked for several hours before she announced she was going to turn in. She had to be awake early in the morning for an aerobics class she was leading at Avenue Fitness. She told Gabe he was welcome to join the class or hang at the apartment and warned him she'd be making coffee at five thirty. Gabe was relieved when he was finally able to settle in for the night on Lucy's futon and take a break from the divorce charade. He wondered how much longer he could manage being on the run and making up stories about himself to tell unsuspecting people like Lucy. Despite the fact that Maria was Raph's sister, Gabe knew it wasn't safe for her to be involved by hiding him. He mulled over possible plans and kept coming back to the idea of leaving town and establishing himself far enough from the D'Angelo family that they wouldn't pursue him. He hated the thought of starting over somewhere far from his hometown, far from Maria, who he still had hopes of re-establishing a relationship with. And even if he could find such a place, the FBI and police were still looking for him. He'd always need to be on the lookout for law enforcement who could come at any time and arrest him. Gabe's fatigue overcame him, and the next thing he heard was Lucy up and puttering around the kitchen.

"Sorry, Gabe. I'll be out of here in a minute." Lucy spooned ground coffee into her drip coffee maker. Now it was clear why Lucy had warned him. The spare room was just a few feet from the kitchen and Gabe could hear everything going on there.

Gabe looked at his watch. It was ten minutes after five. "That's okay. Do you have enough coffee to make one for me?" Gabe said as he stretched his arms over his head on the futon.

"Sure. I'll leave a cup for you on the counter. I'm leaving a stack of newspapers on the counter too. Could you run them down to the recycling bin? It's a big green bin in the alley behind the apartment. Make sure to leave the door unlocked when you go out."

"No problem," Gabe said as he got up and began to find his way to the bathroom wearing gym shorts and a t-shirt. As he passed the kitchen, he saw Lucy carrying a ten-inch stack of newspapers out of the pantry. She had left a folded bath towel and wash cloth for him on the bathroom countertop. Gabe was about to shout a thank you to her when he heard a scream from the kitchen.

"What? Right in my own home?" she shrieked.

Gabe heard Lucy stomp toward the front door and slam the door, then he walked to the kitchen where the coffee was still dripping into the pot. He looked at the stack of newspapers on the counter and saw it. The article, which was on the top of the stack and more than a week old, said that Gabriel Rossi, a former associate of the D'Angelo crime family, was wanted for questioning in connection with a murder in Warminster, Pennsylvania and was considered armed and dangerous. The photo of Gabe wasn't recent, but close enough to his present appearance that Lucy undoubtedly recognized him and realized his story about hiding from divorce lawyers was a lie. He went into the living room and looked out the window onto the street below. Lucy was standing on the corner, half a block away, talking on her phone. Gabe pulled on his jeans and shirt with lightning speed. Grabbing his knapsack, he went out the door, down the stairs to the lobby, and out the back door leading to the alley.

Gabe figured the police would be there in two or three minutes. He entered the alley and went the opposite direction from where Lucy was standing. Fortunately, it was also the most direct route to his car. He turned right on the street that the alley crossed and sprinted to his car which, as far as he knew, Lucy had not seen. In a few minutes, he was driving out of the area and had not heard any police sirens. Knowing he needed to lay low for a few hours, he drove north until he came to Wissahickon Valley Park, where he had evaded Phil and Denny a few days ago. He parked the car in a small lot by a trailhead and put his duffle bag in the trunk. He swung his knapsack containing water, some protein bars, and various other items over his back and headed south on the trail. It was his favorite trail for running and one of the most beautiful trails in the park along the Wissahickon Creek.

After about an hour of brisk walking, he came to a rocky trail that took him up a hill, walking parallel to Wissahickon Creek. In another half hour, he arrived at his destination, the Devil's Pool. He was able to work his way down from the high ground to the actual pool. The water was unusually low in the tributary that flowed into the pool, but it was still full. Gabe couldn't help but think back to the times he dove into the cool water after a run in hot weather. The air was fresh, and buds were starting to blossom into leaves on the trees. If only he could live in a world as peaceful as the surroundings where he found himself now. Gabe stretched out on a large, flat rock, placing his knapsack under his head like a pillow. As he stared at the canopy of trees above, he listened to the birds chirping and the gentle sound of water passing over the rocks in the stream.

He could not shake his troubled feelings and wondered where to go and what to do next. Should he contact the lawyer he had used in the criminal trial a few years ago? Once he did, the lawyer would push Gabe hard to turn himself in, as no lawyer wanted to be accused of harboring a fugitive. Even if exonerated from the murder in Warminster, Gabe knew he'd be facing some time in prison for violating his parole. Maybe he could negotiate time in one of the federal minimum-security prisons where he would be reasonably safe from any inmates who might be indebted to the D'Angelo family and willing to carry out a hit against him. It wasn't an empty hope, since he still had lots of information he hadn't given to the feds yet, including the records Gabe had kept that incriminated Raph in illegal gambling operations. And then there was the video of Phil Morino threatening Maria to find out where Gabe was staying and linking Morino to the break-in and beating of Brian. Gabe felt sure Maria would cooperate and testify against the men who came to her home and threatened her. Gabe took a deep breath and closed his eyes. In a few moments, he drifted off to sleep.

CHAPTER 45

Raph sat in his home office with Gus Nasuti, wondering if he had the right team surrounding him after they had repeatedly failed to find Gabe.

"There's a reason your father had such confidence in Gabe," Gus said. "He was always the smartest one in the room. Don't be discouraged. We'll find him sooner or later, unless he decides to leave town, which would also solve our problem."

"How would that solve our problem?" Raph asked with an edge in his voice. "Even if he leaves, he could come back at any time. How would that look to our crew? It would look like we're a bunch of idiots, which seems pretty accurate right now."

Just then Raph's phone buzzed. It was a local policeman named Harvey Caldwell who was on the D'Angelo payroll.

"Raph, it's Harvey."

"Yeah Harvey, what's up?" Raph asked.

"We got a call at the precinct in Germantown about a sighting of Gabe Rossi."

"When?" Raph asked, suddenly very interested in the call.

"Just now. Apparently, he was staying with some fitness trainer who lives in an apartment near the corner of Church Lane and Germantown Avenue. The bulletin says she recognized his picture in an old newspaper she had and left the apartment. The precinct sent a car over and he was already gone."

"Anybody see him or where he went?"

"Only the woman, but she didn't see him leave. We've got a bulletin out for everyone in a three-mile radius to be on the lookout."

"Does Rossi have a car?" Raph asked.

"Beats me. The bulletin says he could be on foot or in a vehicle," Caldwell replied.

"Thanks, Harvey. Keep me posted." Raph looked at Gus. "You see? He's been hiding right under our noses. That was Caldwell, and he got a bulletin that Rossi was in Germantown just a few minutes ago. He was staying with a woman who called the police when she realized Gabe was wanted for questioning."

"So he got away from the police?" Gus asked with a slight smirk.

"No, he was gone before the cops got to her apartment."

"So what do we do, get some crews driving around there?"

Raph sat with his elbows on the armrests of his chair, putting his hands under his chin. "I bet I know where he is."

"So, what about my question? Do we get some crews on this?" Gus asked again. "And you and I go find him where you think he is?"

"You stay here and organize the crews. Put more on the north side of Germantown. I'm going to go by myself to the spot where I think he is. I'll call you if I need you."

"You sure that's a good idea? If you're so sure he's there, he may be expecting you."

"Just leave it to me. We've tried the usual approach, and it hasn't worked. I'll call you if I need help." Raph reached in his drawer and removed a compact Glock. He snapped a magazine into it and tucked the gun in his belt as he stood up and headed outside to his car.

CHAPTER 46

Maria was teaching Monday morning, but she was having trouble concentrating because she was so worried about Brian. She finally had a free period at ten o'clock. She walked to the faculty break room, which was empty. Being too impatient to wait until the afternoon, Maria pulled out her phone and called Brian's room at the hospital. She let it ring about twenty times, but no one picked up. *Why isn't he back in his room?* She frantically redialed the hospital number and asked for the nurse's station near Brian's room. After being placed on hold for about three minutes, she hung up and called the main number again. The switchboard answered on the third ring. When they attempted to patch her through to the nurse's station, the phone rang and rang. Finally, someone picked up.

"Oncology Department."

"Is this the nurse's station for room 403?" Maria asked.

"Yes, may I help you?"

"I'm trying to reach Brian Murphy in 403, but he's not picking up the phone."

"Let me connect you to his nurse."

"Could I just ask—" Maria started to say, but heard background music as she was put on hold.

Nervous and frustrated, Maria began to pace back and forth in the faculty lounge. She looked at the clock; she had already spent more than ten minutes being shuffled around and on hold. She needed to get back to her classroom and refresh her mind on the lesson plan for the next period. She put her phone on speaker so she could put it down on the table, sat down, and put her head in her hands, taking deep breaths to calm herself. The music continued, and she considered hanging up and calling later, but felt she would have wasted all the time she had already spent trying to get through to somebody.

She got up and began pacing again, then stopped to look out the window. There was a boys' softball game going on for physical education class. She could see Vince Kilmer, the PE teacher, blowing his whistle and telling the boys to fall in and line up to return to the locker room. Maria would need to wing it in her next class if she didn't return soon to look at her notes. She hadn't taught the lesson in a year. She was just about to disconnect when the music stopped and a voice came on the phone.

"This is Aleksandra," the new voice said. Maria detected a slight Russian or Eastern European accent.

"I've been trying to reach Brian Murphy. Are you his nurse?"

"Yes, I'm his nurse. He's out getting some tests," Aleksandra said.

"He was supposed to have an MRI first thing this morning. Why is it taking so long?"

"I'm not supposed to give out information on the phone. Are you a family member?"

"I'm his fiancée."

"He had the MRI earlier today and they've sent him for some more tests."

"Is he doing okay?"

"Again, there's not much I can tell you. Why don't you call his room in an hour. He should be back by then."

"Okay, thank you," Maria said and hung up. She picked up her purse and was about to head back to her room when her phone rang.

She shook her head in frustration, all but giving up on going over her lesson before the kids came back in about twenty minutes. She was teaching sixth grade social studies focusing on ancient civilizations. Today was supposed to be an important lesson on the ancient Babylonians.

When she saw the call was from Rose, she forgot about class and picked up. "Rose, is everything okay?"

"Maria, I'm worried about Raph. He left in a big hurry yesterday, and I expected he wouldn't be home until late, but he came back in the afternoon and locked himself in his study. This morning, he was in the study again with Gus Nasuti until he left again and jumped in his car. Something is going on, and I don't have a good feeling about it. By the way, I really missed you last night, but I understand why you couldn't come."

"I'm about to go into class, but I'm sure everything will be okay. My father was in and out a lot and we kind of got used to it. If you like, I can call you later, but right now I need to get back to my class."

"Okay, thanks for taking my call. It's always good to hear your voice. Oh, one more thing. Have you heard from Gabe? I think this has something to do with him."

"I haven't heard from him in a few days. Actually, I'm trying to get away from the situation," she said, not wanting to add details about the danger of crossing Rose's husband, Raph. "I'm in a rush and can't talk now, but I'll be on lunch break from about twelve thirty to one fifteen. You can call me then to talk more if you like. I'm waiting to hear from Brian since he's getting a bunch of tests done this morning."

"Oh my gosh, I'm sorry. It slipped my mind that you'd be trying to speak to Brian. I hope he's okay. Look, maybe we can talk tonight if that's easier," Rose said.

"Take care, Rose," Maria said as she walked back to her classroom to use the last ten minutes of her break to skim through the lesson plan.

CHAPTER 47

Whether it was nervous exhaustion from life on the run, or the fresh air in the park, Gabe had slept for nearly two hours on the large, flat rock alongside Devil's Pool. When he began to wake up, he heard what sounded like footsteps on the loose rocks surrounding the pool. *It's probably just the noise of the forest,* he thought. The next sound, however, was unmistakable: It was the sound of someone pulling back and releasing the slide on a semiautomatic pistol. Gabe tensed, opened his eyes, slowly lifted his head, and realized he was staring down the barrel of a Glock.

"I knew you'd be here," Raph said. "Your girlfriend in Germantown called the cops and they were hot on your trail. This was as good a place as any to lay low for a while."

"She's not my girlfriend. She's just a friend who let me crash for the night." This fact meant nothing to Raph, but Gabe knew he was in a very dangerous situation. If he could keep Raph talking, maybe he would have second thoughts, or Gabe could figure out a way to extract himself from the situation.

"She can't be much of a friend if she called the police." Raph laughed.

Gabe knew he had little chance of escaping. He had spent time at the shooting range with Raph and knew he wasn't a skilled marksman, but it was hard to miss someone lying on the ground six feet away. If there was some way he could get up and make a run for it, he might make it; Raph would have trouble hitting a moving target even at close range.

"Well, I didn't say she was a close friend. I think she figured out there were some holes in my story," Gabe said.

"Holes in your story aren't the only holes you're going to have."

"What about the holes in *your* story?"

"What holes?"

"How did the Carbones figure out where Maria was before everything went down? It wasn't well known that she was at a convent in Lindenwood. And how did the FBI know to follow the Carbones to the safe house where I was protecting Maria? Was it a scheme to get me arrested so I'd have no choice but to testify against your father? The whole thing ended with you being head of the D'Angelo family. Sounds pretty convenient to me."

Raph stepped back a few feet and shook his head. "Not that again. You don't know what the hell you're talking about."

Gabe slowly sat up, propping himself up with his arms on the flat rock. He wasn't there yet, but his plan was working. He was one step closer to standing, and Raph was a few feet further back.

"Raph, when I had a meeting with Hank Maranzano a few weeks ago, I learned a few things about the incident at the safe house and what led to it. He didn't like the way Bruno Carbone handled the situation and he had no hesitation about spilling the beans. Like I told you before, Hank said you tipped them off about where Maria was, and he implied that you tipped off the FBI as well."

"Hank never liked me. Of course he's gonna tell you a story about me, but he's still full of shit."

Raph had lowered his arm holding the gun. He was still in a position to raise it and shoot Gabe at close range, but the situation was improving. "And what about the fact that I spared your life twice when I could have easily killed you. Doesn't that count for something? I could have easily killed you in the barber shop and gotten away. The FBI would have been relieved to cross another mafia boss off their list."

"You know the rules. You broke the code of silence, then you came out of witness protection. You should have stayed hidden. But I'm curious. You said 'twice.' What was the other time?" Raph asked.

"Somehow you guys found me at the shrine in Barto. When I got away, you thought you were following me. But I had pulled off the road and ended up following you all the way back to your home in Chestnut Hill. It wasn't the first time I followed you home, but this time you were there unguarded, and I was only a few feet away. I could have easily shot you."

"Doesn't matter, Gabe. Like I said, you know the rules." Raph raised the pistol again and aimed it at Gabe, who was still sitting on the ground with his legs crossed.

Gabe knew his time was running out when he saw something out of the corner of his eye. Gabe didn't turn his head for a better look; he knew every second counted and he kept eye contact with Raph.

Raph pressed his lips together and squinted, preparing for the loud report of his gun, when a voice behind him shouted ,"Drop the weapon!"

Three FBI agents had quietly moved into position behind Raph and had their weapons trained on him. Raph instinctively turned around with his arms extended and the gun raised in shooting position, pointed at the closest agent, whose gun rang out with a shot, dropping Raph to the ground.

Agent Natalie Perez, who had fired the shot, quickly approached Raph to assess his injury. He was alive, but bleeding from the upper right side of his chest. She kicked Raph's gun out of his reach and turned toward one of the other agents. "Andy, bring a trauma kit over and check this guy out. I believe we have Mr. Rafael D'Angelo here." She turned toward Gabe, still sitting on the ground. "You, on the ground, put your hands behind your head. Mac, check him for weapons."

Agent McIntyre approached with his gun trained on Gabe. Agent Perez pressed a button on her shoulder mic. "This is Special Agent Perez. We have one suspect down from a gunshot wound and another in custody. We need an ambulance and backup at a spot near the Forbidden Drive Trail, about a mile below the Bells Mill Road access to the park. Subject to further identification, I believe the man down is Rafael D'Angelo," she said, knowing the mention of Raph's name would shift the whole operation into high gear. "I believe the subject in custody is Gabriel Rossi, who has an outstanding warrant for violation of his parole.

"Gabriel Rossi?" Agent McIntyre said as he stood in front of Gabe still sitting on the ground.

"Yes, that's me. Tell them you're at the Devil's Pool. That will pinpoint your location."

"Keep quiet and only speak if we ask you a question," Agent McIntyre said. "Now lean forward slowly and raise yourself up so you are on your knees and then put your hands on your head." McIntyre skillfully checked Gabe for weapons. "He's clean."

For a split second, Gabe feared the agent would find his pistols, which would have subjected him to new felony charges. Then he remembered that he had left them in the duffle bag in the car. Neither the car nor the guns were traceable back to him since they weren't registered in his name and he was in the habit of wiping everything down regularly.

"Good. Bundy, what's his condition?" Agent Perez asked the other agent who was still working on Raph.

"Looks like a through-and-through shot to the right side of the subject's chest. I've reduced the bleeding, but now it depends on how quickly we can get him to a hospital."

Agent McIntyre had cuffed Gabe's hands behind his back. He grabbed him by the arm to help him stand and turned him to face Agent Perez.

"Gabriel Rossi, you are under arrest for violation of parole conditions, pursuant to a warrant issued by the Federal District Court for the Eastern District of Pennsylvania," Perez said. The loud sound of a helicopter flying directly overhead interrupted the recitation of his rights. "There's a chopper right above us. Is that one of ours?" Perez asked into her radio. "Okay. Let's put a rush on getting some EMTs out here. The man down is seriously injured."

Perez returned her attention Gabe. "We've been looking for you."

"So has everybody else," Gabe replied. "I'm glad you came when you did, because Raph didn't meet me here for a social call."

"You want to tell me how you came to be at Devil's Pool with Mr. D'Angelo pointing a gun at you?"

"I think it's obvious what Raph was doing here. But I'd like to speak to my lawyer before going into detail. Let's just say that I've got some evidence you'll be very interested in."

"Fair enough," Perez answered.

Chapter 48

Maria had finished her last class at two thirty and was gathering her things to go home, where she would finish preparing for tomorrow's lessons. She was amazed at how well the class went after lunch in view of her shortened prep time and thought maybe she could get by with less preparation in the future. Just as she was wondering if she could get a call through to Brian, her phone rang. When she saw the call was from Jefferson Hospital, a shiver ran up her spine.

"Hello, this is Maria D'Angelo," she answered, not knowing who was making the call.

"It's me," Brian said.

"I tried to call earlier but they said you were out for some more tests. So how is everything?" she asked with concern in her voice.

"The doctor was just in and he said there are some lesions on my spine in my neck. He said it looked like they could have come from the tumor in my brain."

"It sounds like he wasn't sure."

"That's right. He said the only way to tell was to do a biopsy and he didn't think that was worthwhile until after my surgery. He said the priority is to remove the tumor," Brian said, his voice catching on the last few words.

"You poor thing. I've been very worried, but I'm sure things will get better. I know you've got some great doctors there, and they'll do what's best. I'm praying for you constantly," she said. "Is there any news on the surgery?"

"They were originally thinking Wednesday, but they've moved it up to tomorrow morning. I guess that means they're pretty concerned about it."

"Oh Brian, maybe I should come down tonight."

"Thanks for offering, but they're going to be in and out of my room doing more prep. They said I'd be taken down to the OR by seven tomorrow morning."

"I should be there with you tomorrow. I can take the day off," she offered.

"No, please don't. I'll be in surgery and recovery most of the day. I'd feel better knowing that you're doing what you do best—teaching your students. Maybe you can come by tomorrow evening. In fact, I can't think of anything that would cheer me up more after surgery than seeing you," Brian said. "It will be something for me to look forward to."

"Okay, it's a date. I'll be there tomorrow evening. Is there anything I can do for you until then?"

"No, I'm fine. Oh, some orderlies are here to do some test. I think it's an EKG, so I'd better hang up."

"Brian, take care. I'll be thinking and praying for you until I see you. Again, if there's anything you need, let me know." They said their goodbyes and disconnected.

Although Maria's time at the convent was cut short, she remembered much of what she had learned there. She was worried for Brian, but she felt a sense of peace knowing they were both in God's hands. Maria recalled one of her favorite verses from the Bible, from the epistle to the Romans: "We know that in all things God works for the good of those who love Him, who have been called according to His purpose." That verse had never meant so much to her as it did now.

As Maria walked to her car, her phone rang again. This time it was Rose. She was tempted to decline the call in light of all that was on her mind relating to Brian, but she accepted.

"Maria! Oh I'm so glad you're there!" Rose shrieked.

"What is it, Rose?"

"It's Raph. He's been shot!"

"What? What happened? Is he okay?"

"I just got a call from somebody, I don't even remember who. He's in critical condition at the Chestnut Hill Hospital. That's all I know. I don't know who did it or how it happened. But you're his sister, so I wanted you to know."

"Are you at the hospital?" Maria asked.

"No, I'm home. Maria, I don't know what to do!"

"How about if I come over and we can figure out what to do together. Maybe we should go to the hospital. I can drive you," Maria offered trying to sound calm.

"Oh, thank you so much. That would be great."

"What about Tessa?" Maria asked. "I'm not sure she should come to the hospital now."

"You're right. I'll see if I can get her sitter to come. I'll just tell Tessa that Daddy's in the hospital and it's not the time for children to visit or something like that."

"That sounds good. I was actually in my car when you called so I'll head over now. I should be there in twenty minutes or so."

As soon as she ended her call with Rose, Maria turned on the local radio station. The shooting of Rafael D'Angelo was the top headline. The reporter said Raph was shot in Wissahickon Valley Park while resisting arrest by the FBI. He was in critical condition at a local hospital. A wave of worry swept over Maria as she wondered if Gabe was involved in the gun battle. Her fears were soon mitigated when the reporter said the FBI had also taken Gabriel Rossi into custody unharmed. The report went on to say that Gabe was wanted for questioning in connection with a local shooting. Maria had mixed feelings about the news. She was relieved Gabe was okay and that he wasn't the one who shot Raph. At least that's how it seemed. She was sad Raph was injured and in critical condition. After all, Raph was her brother and the father of her niece. But Raph had chosen to live in a world where murders and gunfights were not unusual.

She wondered what the future held for Gabe and Raph now that they were both in custody. At least they would not be trying to kill each other. Maria still had a soft spot in her heart for Gabe and hoped he would come out of this and seek a new life away from mobsters like her brother. After all, that's what Gabe had told her he wanted to do.

Underneath all these thoughts was a dull, sick feeling about Brian's condition. She had done some more research online confirming that the prognosis for people with Brian's condition was not good. On top of that, the lesions they found on his spine made his condition sound even worse. *"In all things, God works for the good of those who love Him,"* she thought.

CHAPTER 49

Rose and Raph lived in the same home where Maria had grown up, and she had gone up the front walkway thousands of times. But this time she was nervous, not knowing how Rose would get through the day's events or what they would find at the hospital. Of course, Maria was also worried about Raph, even though they had been at odds over many things, including Raph's plans for Gabe. When she rang the doorbell, Rose opened it right away. She looked pale and had dark circles under her eyes. Rose was wearing a lightweight fleece jacket and appeared to be ready to leave.

"Hi Rose. Shall we head over to the hospital?" Maria said without even entering the house.

Rose stepped onto the front porch and shut the door behind her without even answering, and the two made their way to Maria's car for the short drive to the hospital. As they drove in silence, Maria debated whether to tell Rose what she had heard on the radio. She decided not to say anything for now.

Rose broke the silence. "I knew something was up. He rushed out of the house with Gus still sitting in his office. I hope to God he didn't go and kill Gabe."

Maria pressed her lips together and decided to tell Rose what she knew. "On the way over, I heard a brief report on the radio that Raph was in the park by Wissahickon Creek, and the FBI shot him while they were trying to arrest him. They said Gabe was taken into custody unharmed."

Rose was silent for a minute before speaking. "It's been like a nightmare the past few days, but now I don't know if the nightmare is ending or just beginning. Raph has done a pretty good job of keeping under the radar, but now that this is in the news, the word is out. I'm the wife of a mobster. That means Tessa is the daughter of a mobster. How will they treat her at school?" Rose started to cry.

Maria didn't have a good answer. "Let's take it one step at a time. I'm sure everything will be okay."

"Thank you. I mean thanks for being with me to help me through this," Rose said, continuing to wipe the tears away with a tissue.

Parking was limited around the hospital, so they had to enter the parking garage and drive up several levels to find a spot. When they got to the main reception area, Maria noticed a large number of people sitting in the waiting area, some with cameras and recording equipment. She took the initiative to speak first, in a soft voice.

"We'd like to find the room where Rafael D'Angelo is."

"You and everybody else," the receptionist said. "He's in intensive care, and I'm not sure you'll be able to visit him. He's technically in police custody."

Maria had been in the same intensive care unit to visit her mother not that long ago, so she knew the lay of the land.

"If we could just get to the small waiting room by ICU, that would be great. I'm his sister, and this is his wife."

"You can try," the receptionist said as she handed Maria and Rose two guest passes to get beyond the reception area.

Suddenly, someone in the reception area shouted. "I think that's his wife!" Numerous people got up and moved toward Maria and Rose. Cameras started clicking and questions like, "Mrs. D'Angelo, how does it feel to be the wife of the mafia leader in Philadelphia?" were shouted.

Maria instinctively grabbed Rose by the arm and shuffled her to an elevator where the reporters couldn't follow since they didn't have passes.

"It's on the main level, one floor up," Maria said. "They won't bother us there."

"I remember where we're going from when we visited Mom last month," Rose said.

When they got to the small waiting room, they hung up their jackets and moved toward the hallway of patient areas. A nurse stopped them.

"It's not visiting hours right now."

"When can we visit Mr. D'Angelo? I'm his sister, and this is his wife," Maria explained.

"I'm not sure. You'll have to ask those two guys." The nurse pointed to two men in suits sitting in chairs outside one of the rooms.

Maria took a few more steps and called to the men in a loud whisper. "Excuse me gentlemen, but this is Mr. D'Angelo's wife, and I'm his sister."

One of the men got up and walked over to Maria. "I'm Special Agent Kirkman, and this is my partner Special Agent Woodley. We're the detail assigned to guard Raphael D'Angelo. He's in FBI custody."

"Can we see him?" Rose asked.

"Technically, I'm not supposed to allow visitors, but you can step in for a few minutes. He's not conscious, so he won't be interacting with you," Agent Kirkman said.

As if on cue, Maria and Rose walked together around a divider that had prevented them from seeing Raph. When they turned the corner Maria stopped dead in her tracks and put her hand to her mouth.

"No!" Rose screamed and slapped her hands against her cheeks.

Raph lay in the bed with his head turned slightly sideways, his eyes closed in a deathly stillness. A breathing tube extending from his mouth was secured with plastic bands wrapped around his head. A sheet was pulled up over his torso, but bandaging over his entire upper chest could still be seen. A spaghetti tangle of wires and tubes led from Raph to various machines and IV bags hanging overhead. The bed was surrounded by multiple monitors displaying every element of bodily data imaginable, while a breathing machine off to the side quietly hummed its rhythmic pulses.

The two women stood in silence as a nurse came in. "Are you supposed to be in here?" the nurse asked.

"Agent Kirkman said we could come in for a few minutes," Maria pointed to the agent, who nodded in response.

"Can you tell us how he's doing?" Rose asked.

"Doctor Damani is right next door. He should be in here in a minute or two."

True to the nurse's word, the doctor came in and approached Raph. He placed his stethoscope on Raph's chest and listened for a moment. As he glanced at the monitors showing his blood pressure and heart rate, Rose repeated her question to the doctor.

"And you are?" he asked with an Indian accent.

"I'm his wife, and this is his sister."

"Give me a moment," the doctor said as he started typing on the computer on a cart near Raph's bed. He turned back and opened Raph's eyelids, shining a small penlight on them. Afterward, he turned to Rose and Maria. "Your husband is a very lucky man. If the gunshot wound had been half an inch lower, it would have severed a major artery in his lung and he would have bled out in minutes. He was in severe shock and lost a lot of blood. He also has some badly fractured ribs."

"Is he going to recover?" Maria asked.

"He's stable. In a day or two, we'll try to wean him off the breathing machine, and hopefully he'll regain consciousness. He may wish he was still unconscious when he tries to breathe with the fractured ribs, but if all goes well, he has a reasonable chance of recovery. But as I said, he lost a lot of blood and he's very weak. There's still a risk of an infection, which would be very dangerous," the doctor said as he turned and made some additional entries on the computer.

"Can we come back tomorrow?" Rose asked.

"That depends on those guys," the doctor said, pointing to the FBI agents.

"Okay. Thank you, Doctor Damani."

Maria and Rose left the patient area and reentered the small waiting room where they had left their jackets.

Rose sat in one of the chairs and put her head in her hands. "I'm so confused, Maria. I just don't know what to do."

"Rose, he's in good hands. It really sounds like he'll be okay," Maria said, hoping to comfort her sister-in-law.

"Yeah, but what about after he recovers? They were arresting him, Maria. He's probably going to prison for who knows how long. Where does that leave me and Tessa?"

"Let's not get ahead of ourselves. You're safe and secure in your home, and I'm sure everything will be okay. Besides, we don't even know what charges they might bring," Maria said. "Have you spoken to Bobby Sandone?" Sandone had represented Maria's father in his criminal trial and was a towering figure in the Philadelphia Bar despite his connection to mob figures. "He'll be able to explain the situation, and he can also explain the trust funds my father set up." She didn't know all the details of the trusts, but she was sure Michael D'Angelo would have made provision to take care of his granddaughter, which would also include taking care of Tessa's mother. That's the way her father was.

"Thanks, Maria. I don't know what I'd do without you," Rose said. "Can I call you later today? Maybe we can come back tomorrow."

"Sure, give me a call. But Brian is going into surgery tomorrow. I plan to go to Jefferson after I'm done at school, so I'll be tied up most of the day."

"I'm so sorry, I forgot. I hope Brian is okay. I'm sure I can pull myself together and drive over here tomorrow by myself. We'll keep each other posted on how our men are doing, okay?" Rose leaned over and hugged Maria.

CHAPTER 50

That night, Maria was so worried about Brian that she barely slept. Rose had called earlier in the evening, but she had no news about Raph. Things weren't much better when she got up and went to teach the next morning. She had a hard time concentrating knowing the doctors were in the process of cutting through Brian's skull to remove a tumor from his brain. This was Maria's fourth year teaching essentially the same materials so she was able to go on auto-pilot using her old notes and lesson plans. She wondered if the students noticed anything different about her.

Maria could hardly believe it when the school buzzer sounded at 11:50, signaling it was lunch time. Maria took her class to the school cafeteria, then retreated to her car to call Jefferson Hospital. She wanted more privacy than the faculty lounge could afford. After a surprisingly short time on hold, she got through to the nurse's station near Brian's room.

"Hi, I may have spoken to your before. I'm Brian Murphy's fiancé."

"Mr. Murphy's still in surgery," the nurse said.

"Any idea when he'll be back?" Maria asked, knowing full well the nurse probably had no idea.

"No, I'm sorry. These surgeries sometimes take a long time. Then he'll be in the recovery room for a while. I suggest you try back around four if you want to speak to him directly. His brother and sister-in-law are here. Shall I try and put you through to the room?"

"Yes, please do," Maria said, not knowing what to think about the fact that Brian had discouraged her from coming to the hospital until after his surgery.

A moment later the nurse came back on the phone. "It looks like they've gone to lunch. Again, why don't you try calling him at four."

"Thanks," Maria said and hung up, knowing she'd be on her way to the hospital by four.

◆　◆　◆

At the end of the school day, Maria headed east on the turnpike to pick up I-95 to take her into the city. When she got to the interstate, traffic was backed up. She had assumed most of the traffic would be heading in the opposite direction at that hour, but unfortunately it was backed up both ways. *There must have been a bad accident,* she thought. As she inched forward, her cell phone rang.

"Will you accept the charges for a collect call from the Federal Detention Center in Philadelphia from a Mr. Gabriel Rossi?" the operated asked.

"Yes, of course," she said and waited on hold for about a minute.

"Maria, it's Gabe. Thanks for accepting my call."

"Of course. I was worried about you, but the news said you were in custody and not harmed."

"Yeah, the Feds caught up with me, and it's a good thing they did. They found me right after Raph did in the park. I think if they had come five minutes later, your brother would have shot me. He didn't lower his weapon when they arrived, so they shot him. But you probably knew that."

"Yes, that part was on the news too. Are you okay?"

"Yeah, I'm fine. I'm working with my lawyer to make a deal. If all goes well, I should be out before too long. Are you at home?"

"No. I'm actually in the car heading down to Jefferson Hospital. Brian had surgery today."

"Is everything all right? I mean, is Brian going to be all right?"

"When I called at noon he was still in surgery, so I assume he's in recovery now, maybe even back in his room. It's hard to get information over the phone."

"That's right. You told me about the surgery. I'm so sorry, Maria. I know this is hard on you after all you've been through, so I won't take much more of your time."

"Thanks, but I'm stopped in traffic, so I've got time."

"About the video you sent me of Phil Moreno coming to your house. I'd like to tell the FBI about it, and they may want to interview you so they can understand how it came about. If they can use that information to prosecute Moreno, it will help me get a good deal."

"I guess that would be okay," Maria had no qualms about sending Phil Moreno to prison. *That's where he belongs,* she thought. "Would I need to testify in court?"

"Probably not. If I can provide evidence that Moreno threatened you, that's probably all I will need. It's possible that they will want you to go to court just to prove that the video is genuine. I can have my lawyer explain all of that to you. He would want to talk to you before you talk to the FBI. You can think it over if you'd like."

"Actually Gabe, after what he did to Brian, and the threats he made to me, if I can help put him away for a long time, I'm on board."

"Thank you so much. That means a lot to me."

"I don't know how much longer I can talk. I'm in heavy traffic on the interstate. But could this blow back on my brother? I mean, I assume they're going to bring charges against him."

"I was going to get to that. I've got separate evidence about your brother's involvement in gambling and sports betting that wasn't on my laptop when the FBI arrested me. That will be part of my deal with the government. Are you okay with that?"

"Yes," Maria said. "I've given it a lot of thought. Raph is family, but whatever charges they bring against him, it's his own doing. I think he needs to face the consequences. I told him to leave you alone and he ignored me. So, yes, I'm okay with you using any evidence you have against Raph."

"Thank you again, Maria. You're one of the best friends I ever had."

"Is the FBI going to ask about how I helped you hide?" Maria asked.

"I don't know what they're going to ask, but I will never say a word about that. They can lock me up and throw away the key, but I will never answer questions about you helping me. I've got some really great evidence to share, and we will make it a part of the deal that you are off limits, other than to prove the video of Moreno is genuine."

"Okay. The traffic is starting to move and I need to concentrate on getting to the hospital. Thanks for calling. I'm glad you're okay."

"Thank *you*, Maria. And I hope Brian is doing better."

◆　◆　◆

As Maria headed toward Jefferson Hospital, it was full-on rush hour, and she found herself sitting at successive traffic lights as she attempted to navigate the streets around the sprawling urban hospital. Chestnut Hill Hospital and its surroundings, where her brother was, seemed like a quaint suburban village by comparison. She wondered whether it would have been easier to travel to the city by train. She eventually arrived at the parking garage, found an empty spot, and breathed a sigh of relief when she finally entered the main lobby of the correct building and took the elevator to Brian's floor.

"Excuse me, is Brian Murphy back from surgery?" Maria asked the woman at the closest nurse's station. She wanted to make sure it was okay to visit him and was anxious for any information she could get.

"Yes, he's back. I think some family members are with him now. You can go in and see him if you'd like."

"Do you know how everything went?" Maria asked.

"You'll have to speak to the doctor about that. He'll probably be back later this evening to check on Brian."

Maria was nervous as she walked down the corridor to Brian's room. She noticed how quiet it was compared to the hustle and bustle of the other parts of the hospital she had passed through. When she entered the dimly lit room, she took a deep breath and put her hand to her mouth as she saw Brian stretched out on the bed, with his upper body slightly elevated. His eyes were closed, and he had bandaging covering the entire top of his head. He had tubes wrapped around his head to deliver oxygen to his nose, and there were black and blue marks on the side of his head just below the bandages. A lump formed in her throat as she saw the man she had planned to marry unconscious and looking totally helpless and vulnerable. Maria hardly noticed that Brian's brother, Mike, and his wife, were sitting off to the side.

"Hi, Maria," Mike said. "You've met Hillary, my wife, I think."

"Hi. How is he?" Maria asked, seemingly ignoring the reference to Mike's wife.

"He got back an hour ago, but he's been sleeping. Apparently, he woke up in the recovery room but he fell back asleep."

"Did you see the doctor yet?"

"Yes. He was here about a half hour ago. He said Brian would be in and out for a while."

"How did the surgery go?" Maria asked, wrinkling her brow.

"The doctor said it went well, but the tumor was deeper than they thought so they weren't able to remove all of it. He said that's not unusual with this kind of tumor."

"So is he going to be all right?"

"The doctor didn't say much. But he did say they had to dig deeper into the area that controls speech. I forget the technical words he used. He said Brian might have some trouble speaking."

"What?" Out of the corner of her eye, Maria saw Hillary put her head in her hands.

"He said it's not unusual. Most patients can improve with therapy," Mike explained.

Maria shook her head. "I guess I wasn't prepared for that."

"The doctor will be back to check on Brian. I'm sure he can answer your questions."

Maria stood by the bed and tried to hold Brian's hand. Mike stepped out of the room and came back with another chair for Maria. As she stood silently by Brian, she closed her eyes and whispered a prayer. She didn't know much about brain surgery, but she knew that the brain is a delicate organ and that cutting deeply, or, deeper than expected, would likely affect not just speech, but other functions as well, at least temporarily. She wondered how Brian would be able to take care of himself when he left the hospital.

As if reading her mind, Mike said, "The nurse told us some patients need to go to a rehab facility after brain surgery. They can help Brian at his own speed with speaking, walking, and anything else if he's having difficulty."

"I'd hate to see him spend time in another institution after being in the hospital. Did the doctor say how long Brian will need to be here?"

"No. But the nurse said most patients with this type of brain surgery are in for five days, maybe a week." The three visitors looked at Brian in silence until Mike continued. "If Brian needs help, I'm pretty limited since I can't get more than a couple of days off work, and I don't know if his insurance would cover nursing care at home for any length of time."

"This summer I'll have time to help him, but in the meantime, I might be able to get him some help at home. I can probably have an answer in a day or two," Maria said.

The three sat quietly, occasionally sharing whispers. A few times, Brian appeared to shift a little in bed or make a sound, but he remained asleep.

"You said they didn't get all of the tumor. What does that mean for his recovery?" Maria asked.

"The doc said he'd be referring Brian's case to an oncologist who will probably want Brian to have radiation or chemotherapy."

"Those both can be very uncomfortable," Maria said, thinking again about how she might get care for Brian in his home. She figured he would need skilled care even if she was available since she didn't know anything about caring for a cancer patient.

At about eight, a nurse came in and reminded the three that visiting hours were over. Mike and Hillary agreed to come back in the morning, but tomorrow they needed to head back to Reading due to their work schedules. Maria, disappointed that the doctor had not arrived in time for her to speak to him, promised to come back tomorrow when school was finished.

CHAPTER 51

"A lot has been going on," Agent Perez said in a hastily called meeting of the Organized Crime Task Force. "The day before yesterday, we took both Raphael D'Angelo and Gabriel Rossi into custody. We had been actively looking for Rossi when we got a tip from a confidential informant that D'Angelo was on the way to find and presumably kill Rossi. Fortuitously, we had several teams, including Agent McIntyre and myself in the area, and we were able to find D'Angelo's vehicle with the help of one of our drones. We tracked him to the north side of the Wissahickon Valley Park, not far from the Valley Green Inn. Unfortunately, Mr. D'Angelo is in critical condition because he turned the gun he was pointing at Rossi toward us and we had to fire on him. At the same time, we were able to take Rossi into custody, and he is currently in the Federal Detention Center."

"How did D'Angelo find Rossi in the park? Was it a planned rendezvous?" Agent Reed asked.

"D'Angelo is not able to talk yet, and when he is he'll be lawyered up, so I doubt he'll have much to say. But from our initial interview, Rossi claims there was no planned meeting and that D'Angelo just showed up and found him," Perez said.

"So it was a chance meeting?" Reed asked.

"The best we can tell is that D'Angelo got wind that Rossi was on the run in the area and he figured Rossi would be at the spot where they used to spend time together."

One of the new agents on the task force, Agent Valerie Harwood spoke up. "So now that we have these two in custody, what happens next?"

"The US Attorney's office is weighing charges against Raphael D'Angelo, not only for his assault of a federal officer and weapons charges, but also charges based on supposedly new evidence from Rossi showing D'Angelo's direct involvement in a sports betting ring. He's also promised a video of D'Angelo's right-hand man, Phil Moreno, threatening D'Angelo's sister. It's a bit complicated, but D'Angelo was apparently convinced that his sister, Maria D'Angelo, knew where Rossi was hiding. Some of D'Angelo's thugs roughed up her boyfriend in Maple Grove and threatened to kill him if she didn't provide information."

"It sounds like Mr. D'Angelo could be going away for a long time," Reed noted.

"That's right. In a week or so, we'll have a better idea of the charges to be brought. Suffice it to say, we're in the process of cutting the head off the remains of the Philadelphi mafia," Perez said.

"What about Rossi? Are they going to bring charges against him?" Agent McIntyre asked.

"The US Attorney doesn't have any new charges against him. However, he was originally sentenced to five years in prison three years ago and he made a deal to get parole after serving a year. Theoretically, he could be forced to serve the remaining years of his original sentence for violating his parole. But I think he's bringing enough to the table to get that reduced significantly. He might even have his parole reinstated without serving any additional time. Again, we'll know more in a week or so."

"What's the status of the murder case in the suburbs?" Agent Reed asked. "Isn't Rossi still a suspect?"

"We're meeting with the Montgomery County District Attorney tomorrow to lay out the evidence we have. It seems clear to us that Rossi was the real target, and that the D'Angelo guys committed the murder while they were looking for Rossi. So I doubt Rossi will be a suspect after our meeting. That murder in Warminster could also come back on Raphael D'Angelo, so again, Mr. D'Angelo is probably going away for a long time," Perez explained.

"Did Ms. D'Angelo help Rossi avoid arrest?" Agent Harwood asked.

"I think that's going to be a non-issue. Assuming Rossi is in the clear on the murder, she can't be held as an accessory to a crime Rossi didn't commit. And my guess is that the US Attorney has no interest in charging her with helping him evade our efforts to bring him in for a parole violation."

"You mentioned that a confidential informant told us D'Angelo was hunting Rossi. Can you provide any more details on that?" Agent Reed asked.

"That information is highly sensitive, and I'm not at liberty to go into those details at this time. But stay tuned, we'll be able to share more details in the future," Perez said as she closed her notebook.

CHAPTER 52

The next day, Maria breathed a sigh of relief when she heard the buzzer signaling the lunch break. The morning had gone quickly, and she had tried not to think too much about Brian. The first thing she did was call Mike after the kids left the room for the cafeteria.

"Hello?"

"Hi Mike, it's Maria. How is everything?"

"He's awake, and they are trying to help him have some lunch."

"But is he doing okay?"

"Yes. They said it would be slow going for a few days. But he's coming around. I told him you'll be in to see him later and he's looking forward to that."

"Could I talk to him?"

"I wouldn't recommend it. It's very hard for him to talk right now. I think it'll be better for you to see him in person. I'll tell him you'll be there soon."

"I probably won't get there until after four. When are you guys leaving?"

"We need to go in about an hour. Don't worry about Brian. He sleeps a lot and he'll probably nap until you get here."

"Thank you, Mike. We'll talk soon about some arrangements I may be able to make to help Brian when he gets home," she said before hanging up. Maria wasn't very hungry, so she went for coffee in the faculty lounge. After she poured a cup, her phone rang. It was another collect call from the Federal Detention Center. She accepted the charges.

"Hi Maria."

"Hello Gabe. Is everything okay?"

"Yes. I'm really sorry to bother you, but I needed to talk to you. Do you have a second?"

"Sure, it's no bother."

"First, how is Brian doing?"

"The surgery went well, but he might have some trouble speaking for a while, which isn't unusual they say. I'm going to the hospital right after school."

"I'm sure he'll be very happy to see you. But to get to the point, I wanted to tell you that things are moving fast here. My lawyer and I met with someone from the US Attorney's office and we have the general outline of a deal. The bottom line is I'm moving to a minimum security facility in Danbury, Connecticut. I will probably be sentenced to be there for a year, but my lawyer says he expects I'll be out earlier if all the evidence I have pans out."

"That's good, I guess. Is that what you were hoping for?"

"It's actually a pretty good result. As I said, I don't think I'll be there the whole time. After that, I can resume my parole in Philadelphia, which is what I really wanted."

"Are you sure you'll be safe here?" she asked, wrinkling her eyebrows as though Gabe were in the room with her.

"I'm not worried about it. They've arrested Phil Moreno on extortion charges, and he's now the prime suspect in the murder. I think you know that your brother is in a lot of trouble too and that he's going to be in prison for a while. Without those two guys in the picture, I think I'm pretty much in the clear."

"I hope you're right," Maria said.

"But the main reason I called is that the FBI isn't going to question you about allegedly helping me. I really didn't think they would, but now it's confirmed. So that's the good news I wanted to tell you."

"What about the police in Warminster who were looking for you?"

"I'm no longer a suspect, and you can't be in trouble for helping me if I didn't commit any crime."

"Thanks. I hadn't thought much about it with Brian being in the hospital, but I really appreciate you telling me," Maria said before taking a deep breath. "Listen Gabe. You told me you were trying to turn the page on some of your past activities. I really hope and pray that this will be a new start for you. I think you're a good man, and I think you'll be good at whatever you put your mind to."

"Thanks Maria. That means a lot." Now Gabe paused. "I hope you don't mind me saying this, but every time I hear your voice, I want to be a better person."

A lump formed in Maria's throat, and tears formed in her eyes. "Thank you, Gabe. I really do believe you're becoming a better man." As she disconnected the call, she wondered how much of those feelings she once had for Gabe might still be there, but she quickly reminded herself that she was with Brian, and he needed her now.

♦　♦　♦

Maria managed to break away early by getting another teacher to handle her last period. This practice was frowned upon, but Maria felt she had good reason. Her early start allowed her to avoid the worst of rush hour traffic, and she pulled into the hospital garage just before four. Ten minutes later she approached Brian's room. The hallway was quiet, just as it was on her previous visit. When she entered the room, no one was present except Brian, who appeared to be sound asleep. They had removed the oxygen tube, which Maria took to be a good sign. She tiptoed up beside him.

"Brian," she whispered. Nothing happened. She whispered his name again and gently touched his arm. This time, he appeared to take a deep breath, and his closed eyes squinted before opening. "Brian, it's me." she said.

Brian looked at Maria and smiled. "Glad you … glad here," he struggled to say, taking another deep breath.

Maria leaned in and kissed him on the cheek. "How are you feeling, darling?"

"Be-er."

"That's okay. I understand. I got here as quickly as I could after school. I hope you weren't lonely this afternoon."

Brian shook his head once. "Slept."

"That's good. I'm sure rest is the best thing for you right now. Did you hear the news? My brother is in custody. Actually, he's in the hospital in Chestnut Hill. He was wounded when the Feds arrested him. He's stable, and the doctors think he'll be okay. They took Gabe into custody at the same time. He wasn't injured." Maria said, sparing Brian the details of Raph being caught when he was about to shoot Gabe.

"Worried for Ra … Raph?" Brian asked.

"I'm more worried about Rose and Tessa. It's going to be hard on them if Raph goes to prison. I mean, not financially hard, they'll be provided for. It's just the idea of having your husband or father sent away to prison." Maria paused and looked out the window. "I can get you help … I mean when you go home. If you need any help until you are fully recovered, I can get Henry to come and stay with you."

Brian gave her a puzzled look.

"Henry is who took care of my mother before she died," Maria explained. "He actually had a room in her condo. He took care of cleaning, shopping, cooking, and whatever else needed to be done. He also drove her to doctors' appointments. I don't think you'll need him very long, but he's available."

"Sounds expen … expensive," Brian said.

"Don't worry about that part. It will be taken care of. Just focus on getting yourself better. I'm sure you'll be up and around in no time. Maybe you won't even need Henry, but I think you might appreciate him the first week or so that you're home."

"Tired." Brian blinked his eyes several times.

"That's perfectly all right. Get some rest. I'll be right here." Maria had planned on staying until they made her leave at the end of visiting hours.

Brian's nap was short-lived. He woke up in about ten minutes.

"Still here?" he said.

"I told you I wasn't leaving."

Brian reached for Maria's hand. He held it, resting his forearm on the edge of the bed. "Something … to ask you."

"Yes, what is it?"

"Mah … marry," he said, pulling her hand closer.

"Are you proposing to me?"

Brian nodded yes, with a sheepish grin.

Maria look into his eyes and smiled as she leaned in and kissed him. "Of course I will. I thought you'd never ask!"

CHAPTER 53

Two weeks later, Maria's car approached Brian's home in Maple Grove on a Saturday morning. She had planned to spend the day there, giving Henry the afternoon off. Things were going well, and Brian was up and around and doing much better. He had been seeing a speech therapist at Abington Hospital and was making great progress. He was even going to the grocery store with Henry. In another week or two, Brian probably wouldn't need Henry, and with the approach of summer, Maria could be available to help as needed. Radiation therapy was to begin next week, and it remained to be seen what effect that would have on Brian's condition. The radiation was planned not only for Brian's brain tumor, but also for the lesions on Brian's spine where the cancer had spread. The doctors had assured him they would do all they could to make the experience comfortable.

Maria planned to surprise Brian with some plans for their wedding, which they were hoping to hold in a couple of months, maybe late June or July. Maria knew she and Brian might not have much time together and she wanted the wedding to be special. The surprise was that a family from church were members of the Huntingdon Valley Country Club and had offered to make one of the larger club rooms available for the wedding reception, with Maria and Brian only having to pay for the food. It would not be inexpensive, but Maria could draw funds from the trust her father had set up for her. They were planning to hold the ceremony at Saint Bart's Church, where they attended, but they had the option to hold it on a patio overlooking the golf course at the country club.

Most of the guests would be friends from the schools where Maria and Brian taught. Neither one had many family members available to come. Brian's brother and his wife and Brian's elderly mother were the only members of his family on the list. Maria's only family members on the guest list were Rose and Tessa. In fact, she asked Rose to be her maid of honor. Had he been available, Raph would have made the guest list as he was Maria's closest living relative, but even though he was expected to recover, he would still be in custody awaiting trial on serious felony charges. Before Maria's father went to prison, her wedding would have been a huge affair held in a cathedral, with politicians, public figures, and members of Michael D'Angelo's criminal organization; it would have been a feature story in *The Philadelphia Inquirer*. Just thinking about that made her breathe a sigh of relief that she had escaped that world.

Maria was growing more excited as she turned the corner onto Brian's street. She could hardly wait to see the look on his face when she told him about the venue for the reception. But up ahead, she saw a what appeared to be a truck and a police car parked in front of Brian's house. As she approached, she realized the truck was an ambulance. She pulled as close as she could, jumped out of the car, and ran to the house. Henry stood on the front porch talking to one of the EMTs.

"What happened?"

Henry turned toward her. "Brian took a fall. I was headed toward the stairs to help him come down and he tried to go down by himself." Anticipating Maria's likely question, he continued. "I told him not to try the stairs on his own, but you know Brian. He can be stubborn."

"Is he okay?"

"I don't know. Fortunately, he fell near the bottom, but I think he bumped his head. He wasn't conscious when I got to him. He started to come to, but I couldn't get much of a response, so I called an ambulance."

"Can I see him?" Maria asked.

"I doubt it," Henry said, shaking his head. "They kicked me out. They're busy checking his vitals, then they're going to load him up for the ride to the hospital. They said they're concerned about moving him since he bumped his head so soon after part of his skull had been removed and put back."

Maria ignored Henry and pushed past him into the house. There were several medical technicians hovered around Brian and they appeared to be talking to him. Then she realized they were on a call with the hospital. The person closest to Maria was standing next to a laptop on the countertop in Brian's kitchen. Maria tapped him on the shoulder.

"I'm Brian's fiancée and also one of his caregivers. Is it okay for me to be here?"

"It's okay ma'am. We just wanted to limit it to the closest family members."

"How is he doing?"

"He took a bad fall, and we're on the phone with the ER at Abington Hospital. It looks like we'll be taking him there for a preliminary evaluation. The ER already has his records from Jefferson, and they'll be talking to Brian's surgeon. Are you Maria?"

"Yes. Why do you ask?"

"He's been asking for you."

Maria closed her eyes and took a deep breath. "Please can I see him now? I think it will help if he knows I'm here."

"Yeah, sure. Just let our techs finish up and you can speak to him."

Maria watched all four EMTs gently lift Brian onto a stretcher that had been collapsed down to floor level. After they raised it up so it could be wheeled to the ambulance, the lead tech motioned her to come beside the stretcher. Brian's neck was secured in a brace so he couldn't turn his head. Before his fall, Brian's bandages had been removed, revealing a shaved head with a large scar where the surgeon had opened his skull to reach the tumor. He wore a ski cap most of the time to cover up his scar. Since the fall, a new bandage had been placed around his head and a small amount of blood was leaking through. Maria approached and leaned over him, silently gasping when she saw the newly bandaged wound.

"I'm here Brian. How do you feel?" she asked softly.

Brian's eyes turned toward her and she saw him attempt to force a smile. "My head hurts really bad.

"I'm so sorry, dear. I'm here with you now. They're going to take you to the hospital to check you out. I'm sure they'll give you something for the pain. I'll follow you over so I can stay with you" Maria took Brian's hand and squeezed it. She felt Brian's weak grip as he tried to squeeze back.

"We need to get him to the hospital," one of the EMTs said in an effort to get Maria to stand back.

Henry came into the house and stood behind Maria. "How's he doing?" he asked.

"He's awake and in some pain. I guess we'll know more after they check him out at the hospital. I'll be following them over."

"Do you need me to come?" Henry asked.

"Not right now. I think it'll be hectic for a while at the ER. Why don't you straighten up here and stop over in a little while. Maybe we'll know more by then." Maria really wanted to be alone with Brian at the hospital; the instructions to straighten up were really just an excuse to keep Henry at the house for a while. "If they keep him overnight, I might need you to bring some stuff."

"I'm really sorry about this. I should have made sure he wasn't going to use the stairs."

"It's not your fault. We both told him not to use the stairs. When Brian has a mind to do something, there's usually no way to stop him."

"I can see that," Henry answered.

◆　◆　◆

"Ms. D'Angelo?" a nurse said, looking around the waiting room. Maria stood up. "You can come back now."

Maria had been sitting in the waiting room for almost an hour. She walked through an automatic door and along a row of beds separated by curtains until she came to Brian, who was lying with his upper body slightly elevated. His head had been rebandaged, and he had an intravenous tube in his arm, covered with tape.

Maria stood next to the bed. "How are you feeling?"

"Still a little woozy," Brian said. "They did a CT scan as soon as I got here and they're waiting for the report."

"Did the doctor say anything?"

"He said they want to make sure I don't have any bleeding inside, and they're concerned about damage to where they grafted my skull back in from the surgery. I think they're going to talk to my surgeon at Jefferson."

"Well, I'm sure they will do what's best for you," Maria said, taking his hand into both of hers. "Are you still in pain?"

"It's a little better. They sprayed some stuff on the incision and redressed it, so it's not throbbing like it was. I still have a headache, though. They said they don't want to load me up with medications until they can see if I have a concussion."

Maria thought Brian could use some news to cheer him up. "I've got a surprise for you, darling. Some people at church are members at Huntingdon Valley Country Club."

"That's a pretty swank place," Brian said.

"Well, Todd McDowell is on the board of the club and he's going to make one of the banquet rooms available for our reception."

"How are we going to afford that?"

"That's the surprise. We'll pay for the food, but we're getting the room for nothing."

"How can we afford even the food on two teachers' salaries?" Brian asked.

"Don't worry. I've already spoken to our family lawyer. He said the D'Angelo Family Trust would cover it."

"Are you sure you want to do that? I mean are you comfortable using that money, knowing where it came from?"

"I've thought a lot about that. Right now, I'm the only active trustee. Mom is gone, and Raph can't get any of the money while he's in prison other than his legal fees. Same thing applies to my father. The money is there, more than we could ever use. While I have control, I want put the money to good use. I'm planning to make a gift to a mission hospital in Haiti, and I think our wedding is another good use."

"I guess that's one way to look at it," Brian said.

"So, you don't want to have the reception at the country club?"

"Maria, I'll marry you anywhere you want. I'm okay with the arrangement and I'm glad you're putting the money to good use. I'd hate to think what Raph would do with it if he weren't in custody. Are we having the ceremony there as well?"

"I think I'd rather have the ceremony in the church. That's how I want to start our life together. The club is only about ten minutes away. Are you okay with that?" she asked.

"Of course. Thanks for arranging this."

"Oh good. I've known the McDowells for a long time and I've taught both of their kids. When I told them about our plans, they were thrilled to be able to help us out," Maria said, leaving out the fact that she had also told them about Brian's unfortunate prognosis.

"By the way, I called Mike. He's very concerned, and if they keep you overnight, he'll be down tomorrow."

"I really hate to bother him. I'm sure I'll be okay. Tell him it's really not necessary for him to make another trip."

"Brian, there's no way I can talk Mike out of coming if you're staying in the hospital." Just then, Maria's phone buzzed. "I think it's Rose."

"Go ahead and take it," Brian said as he closed his eyes and appeared to drift off to sleep.

Maria stepped into the hallway to take the call.

"Maria?" Rose asked. "Is everything okay? I tried to call and you weren't picking up."

"I'm at the hospital with Brian."

"Oh my gosh, is he all right?"

"I was on my way to see him and he fell down some steps right before I came. They're making sure he doesn't have a concussion and isn't bleeding around the incision."

"Oh, I'm so sorry. That poor guy, all that he's been through."

"Well, he's awake and alert, and the pain is getting better. I'm pretty sure he'll be okay."

"Look, I'll let you get back to Brian, but I wanted to let you know Raph is getting out of intensive care. I took Tessa to see him. I'm pretty fed up with him but figured his daughter should get to see her father. The doctors still think he's going to pull through."

"I'm glad to hear that. What about—"

Rose interrupted her. "Yeah that's where the news isn't so positive for Raph. The US Attorney is bringing a shitload of charges against him. They're charging him with conspiracy to commit murder in the case in Warminster and a whole bunch of other things. The Montgomery County DA is also filing charges for the murder. The Feds are charging him with extortion for beating up Brian even though he wasn't directly involved. The Philadelphia police are even charging him with the attempted murder of Gabe. I guess they think if they hadn't gotten there in time, he'd have pulled the trigger. Raph's lawyer thinks that's a bogus charge because they can't prove he was going to kill Gabe. Maybe Raph was just trying to scare him. Still, if you add up all the potential sentences, he may never get out."

"Rose, I know you must be devastated. I want you to know that I'm always here for you and Tessa. I'd come right now if it weren't for Brian."

"Thank you, Maria. Numb is probably a better word. I've had it with this life. I'm tired of pretending to be something I'm not, namely, a normal woman in a normal family. Raph brought all of this on himself and if he gets life in prison, he deserves it." Rose paused. "I want out of this lifestyle and out of this marriage. Knowing what I know, I'm sure he was going to kill Gabe."

"Rose, I understand, but don't do anything rash. Let's get together. I'll call you as soon as Brian is out of danger. Maybe we can have dinner. I'd be happy to bring something to your home some evening next week."

"Thanks, Maria."

"I'm serious about not doing anything rash. Keep these thoughts to yourself for now. Raph has some nasty friends, and you shouldn't trust any of them."

"Okay. I'll keep quiet."

"Give Tessa my love. I can't wait to see her."

CHAPTER 54

That evening, Maria sat with Brian in his room at Jefferson Hospital after Brian's surgeon requested that he be transferred to where his surgery had been performed. It had been an exhausting day, and it seemed like they had been waiting forever without getting any answers when a doctor entered the room. They had been hoping Brian's surgeon, Dr. Berenson, would meet with them, but they didn't recognize the doctor who entered the room.

"I'm Doctor Patel," he said. "Doctor Berenson's chief resident."

"Will Brian be able to go home soon?" Maria interjected.

"When Brian fell, he damaged the graft where we repaired his skull after the surgery. We can fix that without too much difficulty, and we're scheduling a procedure tomorrow to do that. We were worried Brian might have suffered a concussion, but fortunately the fall didn't cause any other damage. Because of tomorrow's procedure and the need for the skull to heal, we have to postpone his radiation therapy for at least a week. The news that's not so good is we found some tumorous tissue in the frontal lobe that we didn't see before. It might be new growth, or it might be swelling of the tissue from the surgery. Either way, it's a concern. Hopefully, we can reduce it when we start radiation."

"So how long do I need to stay?" Brian asked.

"Probably another day or two. Then we'd like you to take it easy for another week and come back in for a PET scan to get a full picture of anywhere the metastatic tissue may have spread. Based on the results of that, we'll plan your treatments going forward, which will now include chemotherapy."

"Does Brian need to come here for radiation and chemo?" Maria asked.

"I was just getting to that. There's an excellent oncology group at Abington Hospital. They'll consult with Doctor Berenson and won't do anything different than what we'd do here. In fact, Doctor Kimmel, who leads the group, did a fellowship at Sloan-Kettering, so they are top notch."

After Dr. Patel left, Maria did her best to put on a happy face. It was good news that Brian didn't suffer a concussion, but she was afraid for Brian in the difficult time ahead, with radiation and chemotherapy. If the PET scan showed new areas of cancer, it would only get worse. She began to worry whether Brian would be well enough for their wedding, which was only about six weeks away.

As if reading her mind, Brian spoke. "You know, I want to marry you more than anything in the world, but I've got an ordeal ahead and I don't know how long I'm going to be around. I don't know if I can put you through that and I understand if you want to cancel or postpone the wedding."

Maria pulled out a tissue and wiped her eyes as she leaned forward to kiss Brian gently on his forehead. "Nothing in the world would make me want to postpone our wedding. I'll be right here for you every step of the way, and we'll get through this together."

As Brian closed his eyes, a tear ran down his cheek. "Thank you," he said.

CHAPTER 55

Three months later, Gabe sat in the common area of his cell block at the Danbury Correctional Institution one evening watching a Yankees game with most of the other inmates in his cell block. He had adapted quite well to life at the minimum-security prison. He had been made assistant librarian in the prison's library and had taken up reading in his spare time, something he had not done much of since his high school and college years. When Michael D'Angelo recruited Gabe to work in his organization, he was at Temple University, playing on the tennis team. He used his skill to give tennis lessons on the prison's tennis and pickleball courts. A few of his students paid him in cash, but others paid him in cigarettes. Gabe didn't smoke, but cigarettes were still a common currency for trade at the prison, and Gabe had accumulated a substantial stash that he could trade for special food items, gourmet coffee, and other items that were considered luxuries in prison.

Although the game on television was a good one, with lots of screaming and shouting by the inmates, Gabe's mind was elsewhere. He thought about life after prison and his desire to make a fresh start. He thought even more about Maria and wondered how she was doing. Gabe had heard enough from Maria about Brian's condition to understand that his prognosis was not good and Gabe felt guilty about looking forward to the day in the not-too-distant future when Maria might be available. Would Maria consider getting together with him, he wondered? She had been through a lot in the past few years, and he would need to proceed carefully to win her back.

Gabe's daydreaming was interrupted by a voice behind him. "Rossi, you got a phone call." It was Dominick Luchesi, an accountant who had worked for the Gambino family in New York. Dom had been convicted of filing false tax returns and refused to testify against the Gambino bosses that he worked for. As a result, he was sentenced to six years in prison. Gabe sensed that Dom didn't like him because he had testified against his bosses.

"I thought the phones weren't open this time of night," Gabe said referring to the bank of pay phones that were available for inmates to use certain times during the day.

Dom cocked his head to the right, signaling Gabe to follow. Gabe felt uneasy, fearing he was being led away to be assassinated. He knew Raph still had friends in the prison system, and it wasn't hard to imagine someone owed him a favor, or that Raph had bribed someone to finish the job he had started at Devil's Pool. Gabe quickly thought about how he might escape the serious predicament he was in. If he simply refused to go with Dom, he knew they would find another way to get him alone. Sensing Gabe's hesitation, Dom lifted his hand, revealing a cell phone.

"Here. Take it right around the corner," Dom said. Gabe exhaled, and the two walked a short distance down the hallway, out of earshot of the inmates watching TV. "I'll sit by the TV so you can give me the phone when you're done," Dom said.

Gabe took the phone. "Hello?"

"Gabe it's Gus Nasuti. How is prison life treating you?"

"Just fine, Gus," Gabe said coldly, recalling that Gus had been at the shrine with Raph when he was trying to kill him. Gabe also knew that Raph discussed just about everything with Gus. As a result, he expected Gus to follow up with a threat designed to strike terror in his heart.

"Look, I'm not going to beat around the bush," Gus said in a relatively friendly voice. "You know that Raph is out of commission and probably isn't ever coming back. The other bosses elected me to lead until we figure out who is going take over. I want to let you know that I disagreed with Raph. I told him to leave you alone, but he wouldn't have it. He wanted to make an example of you. Of course I had to go along with his decision."

"That's very comforting," Gabe said with a note of sarcasm. "So you called me just to tell me that?"

"No. I want you to know that you can come back to Philly and nobody will come after you."

"Thanks," Gabe said. Part of him believed Gus, and the other part wondered if it was a trick.

"If you're skeptical about this after all you've been through, I understand. But you have my word that you are safe if you come here. The other bosses feel the same way."

Gus wasn't a saint, but he was a straight shooter, and when he gave his word, it meant something. It's one of the reasons Raph had placed so much trust in him.

"Well, thanks for letting me know. And I want you to know that I hold no hard feelings against you or anyone in the family."

"That's not the only reason I called," Gus said. "Raph used to tell me he thought you were the most talented guy in the organization. You're smart, resourceful, and you can get things done. Gus paused. "With all the recent arrests, we have a shortage of talent. What I'm saying is, we'd like you to come back."

"I'm in prison, Gus. How can I come back?"

"We heard through the grapevine that you're getting out soon."

"I guess word travels fast. But I'll be on parole when I get out. If I make one mistake, including hanging around with the wrong people, I could end up back in prison."

"We could set you up in a legitimate business situation. You're better than most at figuring these things out." There was a pause on the line before Gus continued. "Look, we don't need to discuss details, and I'm not pressing you for an answer right now. We'll talk again."

For a moment, the thought of going back to a job he excelled at in the city he loved was intoxicating to Gabe. He also had a pretty good idea of the talent left in the organization that could lead, and it wasn't much. Maybe Gus wasn't just inviting Gabe to come back, but setting him up to take over. He felt confident that if he played his cards right, he could become the boss in Philadelphia. Gabe was excited at the thought that he could continue the work Michael D'Angelo had begun, moving the business toward legitimacy and eliminating the violence that had plagued it in the past. It would take time and a lot of effort, but he felt it could be done.

Then he thought of Maria. It wasn't a sure thing, but her becoming a widow in the not-too-distant future was a possibility. He could be with her again in every way—or could he? Gabe had all but promised her he would leave behind a life in organized crime. Could he find a way to accept Gus's invitation and still get Maria back?

"You still there?" Gus asked after the long pause on the line.

"Ah, yes. Thanks, Gus. You've really given me something to think about."

"As I said, we'll talk again," Gus said before disconnecting.

Gabe walked back into the common area and handed the phone back to Dom.

About the Author

Tom Morris grew up in Huntingdon Valley, Pennsylvania, a suburb of Philadelphia. He received his BA in Philosophy from Kings College in London, and his law degree from the Dickinson School of Law at Penn State. He practiced law in Philadelphia for seven years and was acquainted with a few lawyers who represented organized crime figures.

He later moved to Florida, where he served as general counsel for Armstrong Global Holdings and was on their executive committee before retiring. He now resides in the Chicago area with his wife, Gwen, and their golden retriever. When he isn't writing, Tom enjoys hiking, fishing, hunting, and reading.